THE BELIAL WITCHES

Book 11 of the Belial Series

R.D. Brady

BOOKS BY R.D. BRADY

Hominid

The Belial Series (in order)
The Belial Stone
The Belial Library
The Belial Ring
Recruit: A Belial Series Novella
The Belial Children
The Belial Origins
The Belial Search
The Belial Guard
The Belial Warrior
The Belial Plan
The Belial Witches
The Belial War
The Belial Fall
The Belial Sacrifice

The Belial Rebirth Series
The Belial Rebirth

The Belial Spear
The Belial Restored
The Belial Blood
The Belial Angel
The Belial Templar (Coming Soon)

The A.L.I.V.E. Series
B.E.G.I.N.
A.L.I.V.E.
D.E.A.D.
R.I.S.E.
S.A.V.E.

The H.A.L.T. Series
Into the Cage
Into the Dark *(Coming soon)*

The Steve Kane Series
Runs Deep
Runs Deeper

The Unwelcome Series
Protect
Seek
Proxy

The Nola James Series
Surrender the Fear
Escape the Fear
Tackle the Fear
Return the Fear

The Gates of Artemis Series
The Key of Apollo

The Curse of Hecate
The Return of the Gods

R.D. BRADY WRITING AS SADIE HOBBES

The Demon Cursed Series
Demon Cursed
Demon Revealed
Demon Heir

The Four Kingdoms
Order of the Goddess

Be sure to sign up for R.D.'s mailing list to be the first to hear when she has a new release!

CAST OF CHARACTERS

The Followers
    Sarah Goode - leader of the Followers, mother of Dorcas
    Susan Osbourne - one of the first arrested
    Rebecca Nurse - seventy-one-year-old grandmother
    Mary Eastly - Rebecca Nurse's sister
    Elizabeth Proctor
    Martha Carrier
    Martha Cory
    Margaret 'Meg' Jacobs - the youngest member of the Followers, George Jacobs's granddaughter

Critical Characters
    Reverend Nicholas Noyes - reverend from neighboring town
    Samuel Parris - reverend of Salem
    Cotton Mathers - leading scholar on witchcraft
    Ann Putnam Senior - mother of Ann Putnam
    Thomas Putnam - father of Ann Putnam
    George Jacobs - Meg Jacobs's grandfather
    Tituba - Reverend Samuel's slave
    George Burroughs - former reverend of Salem

Dorcas Goode - Sarah's daughter

Members of the Court
John Hathorne, magistrate
Jonathan Corwin, magistrate

The Accusers
Elizabeth Samuel - Reverend Samuel's daughter
Abigail Williams - Reverend Samuel's niece
Mary Wolcott
Mercy Lewis
Elizabeth Hubbard
Mary Warren

"Thou shall not suffer a witch to live."
Exodus 22, 18

"If any man or woman be a WITCH, that is, hath or consulteth with a familiar spirit, they shall be put to death."
General Court of the Massachusetts Bay Colony, 1641

"A man also or woman that hath a familiar spirit, or that is a wizard, shall surely be put to death: they shall stone them with stones: their blood shall be upon them."
Leviticus 20, 27

CHAPTER 1

NEWETOWNE, MASSACHUSETTS BAY COLONY

NOVEMBER 1691

Cotton Mather stared out at the crowd that had come to hear him speak. Not yet thirty, his writings on witchcraft and the dangers of their evil for Puritan beliefs and lives had catapulted him into the limelight.

Today he was speaking at the newly created Harvard College. It was only within the last year that they had gotten a house and an acre of land to begin the higher education of men within the New World. The house was in the distance, but the crowd for Cotton's speech was too large for the small rooms inside. Instead, a tent had been erected outside. Fires burned along the edges to keep the attendees warm, but Cotton felt no cold himself. The power of his message kept him warm.

His books and lectures were known throughout New England. And after all the time he'd spent studying and preparing, it was well deserved. For years, he had toiled away, trying to find the topic that would draw people to his lectures. The topic that would make sure they understood the importance of his mind. But finally, on a trip to England, he'd discovered his true calling, his mission, the danger of the Devil among us—the danger of the witches.

Now faces turned up at him. They'd come from all over. From Plymouth and Salem and even as far east as Hartford. His audience sat in rapt attention as he extolled the dangers the witches provided, the signs of their presence among us, and most importantly the way in which to defeat a witch. But now he had a new aspect of this soul-endangering evil that he felt deserved attention.

His deep voice carried over the rows of his audience as he brought his lecture to a close. "Spectral evidence is oftentimes the only evidence available. The Devil is crafty in his approach. He knows he cannot simply leave physical proof behind. So he resorts to an approach that leaves no trace of his wickedness."

He paused, allowing his words to sink in. "But we must be careful to not rush to judge. There must be a fairness in how we approach our subject, for people do tell untruths. It must be remembered, though, that a good and just God would never stand by while a virtuous person is abused. He will always provide a route to vindication.

"But even with God's help, we the virtuous must always be on guard. The Devil looks for our weaknesses, our vulnerabilities. We must stay true to our Puritan ideals, which will see us through these dangerous times."

He kept his frown in place as he delivered his final words. "And remember that there *is* a Devil. It is a thing doubted by none but those that are under the influences of the Devil."

He stepped back from the podium. In his mind he heard the thunderous applause, even though the Puritan nature of his audience would recoil at such an outburst. But he saw the applause in their eyes as they stared up at him in feverish adherence. He spoke the truth. He was the one who would keep them safe.

He nodded and made his way from the tent, stopping to speak with only a few who wished to hear more. Normally basking in the attention after a lecture was his favorite part. But today there was a more important meeting that required his attention. He had uncovered the hints of a coven in the New World. And he would be the one to help bring it to light.

He made his way out of the meeting tent and across the yard. He climbed the cold stone steps, the torchlights beckoning him forward. Pushing open the heavy door, he breathed in the warmth as he slammed the door shut behind him. There was no one about this cold Saturday afternoon. Torches kept the darkness to the corners, but there was still a gloom to the place. He hurried down the hall, making his way to the last door. Pausing, he pulled off his hat, straightening his wig and the collar of his shirt. Taking a breath, he rapped on the door.

"Enter."

Cotton pushed the door open and stepped into the office of the president of Harvard College. "Good evening, Father."

Increase Mather turned, looking down his pointed nose and over his glasses at Cotton. "Ah, Cotton. Good, good. How was the lecture?"

"Well received, I think."

Increase nodded, gesturing for Cotton to sit as he took his own seat behind the large wooden desk, placing the book he had been reading on it. It was a tome on St. Thomas Aquinas. The whole room was filled with such books, which was only fitting for the man who had first received the Harvard Doctor of Divinity degree. "You are making quite a name for yourself within academic circles."

"Yes, Father."

"Now, you said you needed to speak with me about something

urgent? I confess, I am in the dark as to what it might be, and your correspondence did not offer any clues."

Cotton leaned forward. "When I was in England, I came across one of our family's papers. And I learned we were once members of a group known as the Council."

Increase blanched at the name.

"You know of it."

Increase nodded slowly. "Their business is not ours, son."

"Why not? They seem to be trying to track down the truth of our history."

"But not for truth's sake. They seek to make money from the artifacts of the past. Your grandfather would not condone their activities and pulled our family from their ranks. And he made the right decision."

"But, Father, I believe they may be able to help us—"

"No, Cotton. The Council, they are not a force of good. And we should not be part of anything that they are trying to track down. It will only lead to destruction."

"You don't understand—"

"Son, I know you are a man now, but this is not for you. Trust that my father and I know of what we speak and leave whatever it is you think you've found alone."

"But there's a grimoire."

Increase's hand shook as he reached for his handkerchief. "A grimoire?"

"Yes. I was reading in the notes that they believe it was brought to the New World. It is somewhere in New England. And if it is here, that means there is a coven of witches here as well. It is our duty to track them down."

Increase was quiet for a moment before he shook his head. "No. The words of the Council cannot be trusted. Did they call it a grimoire?"

"They said it was a book of immense power. What else could it be?"

"Many things. Do not interfere in this, Cotton. It will not end well." Increase stood up. "Now, your mother has prepared dinner for us."

"Yes, of course," Cotton mumbled. He stood as his father gathered his things from the table behind his desk. What had happened to his father? He had been a shining light in the fight against the Devil. But now age had made him soft.

But Cotton would take up the mantle of the Mather fight. And he would find the unholy coven that had brought the book of the Devil to these new lands.

Yes, he knew his duty. And he would fulfill it.

CHAPTER 2

SALEM, MASSACHUSETTS

LATE JANUARY 1692

Sarah Goode stumbled down the street. Her feet hurt and the morning sickness was making her even more tired. But there were mouths to feed. She spied Patricia Lancaster and Mary Whatley hurrying down the sidewalk toward her. Both wore matching black dresses with similarly dark bonnets. Sarah herself wore a dark gray one that had once been black. But too much wear and too many washings had lightened it over the years.

Pushing aside her nausea, Sarah picked up her skirts and hurried after them. She knew exactly when they caught sight of her. They hesitated, and Sarah knew they were going to try to avoid her. She stepped in their way before they had the chance.

"Goody Lancaster, Goody Whatley. Might you have some coins or food to spare for me and my family?"

Both women looked at each other, their mouths pinched.

Inside, Sarah recoiled at the fact that she had resorted to begging. But her first husband had rung up debts that had followed her into her second marriage, and the inheritance from her father had gone to pay them off. Her husband occasionally tried to get work. But truth be told, he was a horrible carpenter.

"Good Christian women such as yourselves must surely have something you could spare, or perhaps a job?"

Both women cringed, as Sarah knew they would. She had been labeled crazy by the town years ago. It was her own fault. Since she was a child she'd had the gift of sight. Her mistake had been in trying to warn the citizens of Salem when hardship was going to befall them. Instead of heeding her warnings, they pointed to them as proof she had cursed them.

But their silly superstitions could occasionally come in handy. "Of course, if you are not feeling charitable, I may not feel so charitable in my wishes for your future."

"Here." Patricia shoved two coins at her. Sarah took them and looked at Mary, who dropped a coin on the ground. "Take it and be gone." The women stepped around her, pulling their skirts so they did not touch her. Not out of respect, Sarah knew, but to avoid being despoiled by touching crazy Sarah Goode.

Sarah knelt down and picked up the coin. It would be enough for two loaves of bread, maybe some broth. Split amongst the six of them, it would not be much, but she would make it stretch. She stood up, her back protesting, and then the world swayed. She clutched onto the horse railing. Darkness encroached at the edge of her eyes. A vision was coming. Normally she could tell when they would arrive and she took care to make sure she stayed inside. But the babe had made her so sick these last few days that she hadn't recognized the signs.

She stumbled forward and stepped into the alley between the schoolhouse and the mercantile. An old wagon stood waiting to be loaded.

Her legs trembled and her eyesight came and went. *No, not now, please,* she begged as she crawled under the wagon and leaned against the wall of the shop.

No, not now, she pleaded again silently. But as always, the vision did not listen.

CHAPTER 3

Seventeen-year-old Margaret 'Meg' Jacobs walked down the street with her grandfather. It was only the two of them now. Her mother and grandmother had both passed two years earlier from the flu. Meg missed them terribly, but her grandfather was good man, a kind man. She knew the day would come soon when she had to find a husband, and neither of them was looking forward to it.

Two women hurried down the street toward them, their heads bent against the wind. Her grandfather nodded as they came abreast of them. "Sisters Whatley and Lancaster, good morning to you."

"And you as well, Brother Jacobs, young Meg."

"How fare you this morning?" her grandfather asked.

"Well, although we did have to deal with Sarah Goode," Whatley said.

Lancaster shook her head. "The woman is destined for a punishment in the afterlife."

Her grandfather nodded his head, even though Meg knew he did not approve of criticizing Sarah. The woman had a difficult life. "Indeed. She is a poor example of a Puritan."

The women nodded and made their farewells. Meg and her grandfather continued down the street and Meg felt the stirrings of annoyance. She would never say anything to her grandfather, but she hated when their neighbors looked down their noses at those less fortunate. It seemed cruel, unkind.

A swish of grey skirt caught Meg's attention and she glanced up just in time to see Sarah slipping into an alley, her face extremely pale. Meg tightened her grip on her grandfather's arm.

Her grandfather turned his head. "Meg? Is something wrong?"

"No, Grandfather," she said quickly, pulling her gaze from the alley. "I just thought I saw a stray. It looked injured."

He patted her hand with a small smile. "Well, go on. You are too soft hearted. Find me when you are done."

She nodded as he started into the mercantile. "Yes, of course."

She waited until he was inside before hurrying into the alley. It was narrow, only about twenty feet across. The door to the store room for the mercantile was at the back left but no other doors opened into it. The wagon for the mercantile lay sitting near the door waiting to be loaded. The alley led to the stable yard and Meg could smell the horses even from here.

But there was no Sarah. Where was she? Had she already gone? She did not look capable of moving that quickly. A dark shadow shifted under the wagon catching her gaze. Meg gasped and quickly climbed under before anyone saw her. Sarah sat hunched over, her back against the wall, her eyes staring at nothing.

"Oh, Sarah." Meg went to touch her and then drew her hand back. No, best not to waken her. She knew she would come around on her own. Meg glanced around hoping no one came by. She could hear voices in the storage room of the mercantile. *Hurry, Sarah, hurry.*

Sarah blinked and her breath came out in a rush. Her head turned to the side and she frowned trying to focus. "Meg?"

"Sarah, thank goodness. We must go." Meg glanced out into

the alley. Still no one. She crawled from under the wagon, all put pulling Sarah with her and then helped her stand. Quickly slipping an arm around Sarah's waist once she was upright, she hurried them down the rest of the alley toward the stable. She had just slipped around the other end when the storeroom door opened.

Meg let out a sigh of relief. That had been *too* close.

"I must stop," Sarah said quietly.

"Just a little farther," Meg said, hurrying Sarah toward the stable. She opened the door and helped Sarah to a bale of hay before quickly turning back to close the door.

Sarah leaned back against another bale, her eyes closed.

"Sarah, can I get you anything?"

Sarah reached for Meg's hand and gave it a squeeze. "No, child, but I thank you for your help."

"Was it a vision?"

Sarah nodded tiredly.

Meg watched Sarah, noting how pale she looked, how tired. Something had been weighing her friend down these last few months. "You have been having them more often lately, haven't you?"

"Yes, and all of the same thing."

"What is it?"

Sarah opened her eyes. "I must speak with Rebecca and Mary first and then I will share it with all of you. Can you get messages to the sisters? We will need to meet tomorrow night."

"I will tell them."

"Good. You should go. Your grandfather will worry."

Meg knew she was right, but Sarah looked so pale. "I will bring you something to eat. And then—"

"No, Meg. I thank you for your kindness. But even us being seen here is a risk. You must go."

Meg stared at her friend, her teacher, and wanted to stay, but she knew Sarah spoke the truth. Theirs was a burden larger than any one person. Meg leaned forward and kissed Sarah's cheek. "May the Great Mother watch over you."

"And you as well, little sister. Now go, hurry."

Meg hesitated for only a moment before hurrying from the stable. She retraced her steps and was just stepping out of the alley when her grandfather emerged from the mercantile. "Ah, there you are. Any luck with the stray?"

Meg forced her herself to calm down. She shook her head. "No, Grandfather. She was too quick."

"Next time you'll get her. "

"Yes, Grandfather." She fell into step next to him, hoping he did not notice her pounding heart.

CHAPTER 4

The wind was biting and Sarah Goode pulled her cloak more tightly to her. She glanced around, but no one was near. She slipped quietly into the barn on the Nurse plantation, shutting the door quickly behind her.

"Child, you look frozen solid." Rebecca Nurse, portly, with white hair, hustled over to Sarah and clasped her to her chest. "Come to the fire."

Sarah shook her head as Rebecca led her to the flames. "You shouldn't have made a fire. It will draw attention."

Mary Eastly, Rebecca's younger sister by only a few years, added another thick branch to the fire. "The weather will keep people indoors. And you need the warmth."

Sarah couldn't deny it. She let Rebecca lead her over, her toes and fingers tingling painfully as the heat hit them.

Rebecca ran a hand through Sarah's hair. "You cannot continue this way. You and your family should come stay with me."

Sarah shook her head. "No. There is too much at stake."

Rebecca paused her eyes narrowing. "What have you seen?"

"A great deal." Sarah hesitated, once again trying to find any other interpretation for her vision and failing. They had prepared for this moment but at the same time she still could not believe it was here. But ignoring an incoming storm did not make it disappear. It only made the damage worse. "I believe the Council may know the book is here."

Rebecca gasped. "But how?"

The visions of the last few days flew through her mind. At first, the images had been so abstract she hadn't been sure what to make of them. But the feeling that accompanied them had been clear—dread. And today, the final vision had clarified the picture in terrifying detail. "I don't know. But they will stop at nothing to get it. We cannot let that happen."

Mary shook her head. "We knew this time would come, ever since the witch trials in England."

Sarah growled. "Witch *trials*. Stupid people. Persecutions are what they were. According to them, witches are supposed to walk on their hands, ride hyenas, and had pregnancies that lasted for three years. While I admit pregnancy does seem to last for three years, do you truly think those poor women were seen riding hyenas? Those poor people were all killed just to get to us."

"Some of our sisters were caught up as well," Rebecca said quietly.

"I have no doubt." Sarah closed her eyes, weariness falling over her. The babe had been moving a lot today. Her feet ached, and since the vision, a chill had fallen over her skin that the fire's warmth couldn't seem to penetrate. The cold she felt was dwarfed by the knowledge that everything they and their sisters had spent generations protecting was now at risk.

And Sarah knew she was not overemphasizing that risk. She was not known to worry about much, despite the fact that hers had not been an easy life. When her first husband had died, she'd been left with debts and children. The children were a blessing, the debts a curse. One that followed her into her second marriage.

Daniel was not a bad man, but he was not a good one either. And working a full day was a rarity for him. She knew the more you suffered in this life the less likely you suffered in the next, but some days she wished there was a little less to endure now.

"So what do we do now? Do we move on?" Mary asked.

Sarah shook her head. "Where would we move to? The war has brought the boundary of the wild only sixty miles from here. There are not enough cities in this new country to get lost in, and outside the cities is too unsafe."

"We are giving up?" Rebecca asked.

"No. That is not an option either. But they will come for us."

"You've seen it?" Mary asked.

"Just glimpses. I know we are in for a dangerous time. A darkness is spreading. It will cover Salem, snuffing out its light. We must prepare."

Rebecca shared a glance with Mary. "Then we will call all the sisters."

Sarah nodded. "Tomorrow. Meg will let them know. We must plan."

Mary's hand flew to her throat. "That soon?"

"I'm afraid there is no time to lose." Sarah looked at her two sisters of the soul. She had seen more in her visions, but they would provide her two sisters nothing but heartache and fear. Sarah would carry that burden alone. Knowing what she had seen would not stop what was coming. "Tomorrow. We meet tomorrow."

Mary placed an arm around Sarah's shoulders. "You are still chilled through."

Sarah leaned in to her warmth. "I cannot seem to warm today."

"Let me help you." Mary began to rub her arms, and Rebecca placed her shawl across Sarah's legs. Sarah closed her eyes, lest they see the tears gathering there. Her sisters would not survive what was to come.

Neither would she.

But for this one moment, she would let herself enjoy the ministrations of her sisters. Because Mother knew, soon the memory of this moment of love would be all she had to cling to.

CHAPTER 5

The lights to Reverend Samuel Parris's home were shining brightly as he hustled down the street. He'd been meeting with the town council to discuss the new rules. Refugees were pouring in from the French War and the village was struggling under the new burden. That, plus the ever-lingering Indian threat, had set the town on edge.

Samuel knew he was here to guide this flock and show them the way to righteousness. But he couldn't help but think he had some greater purpose than this. A man of his pious nature and adherence to God's rule was meant for more than small-town life.

The night was unusually cool and he was not dressed for it. Shapes moved beyond the front window of his home, and he frowned. Ann Putnam and Mercy Lewis had been over to see the girls earlier, but they should have been long gone by now. And his slave Tituba was not supposed to be in the parlor. That just left his daughter and niece, who was staying with him.

He glared at the offending shadows, his anger rising. If they were still up, they would learn again never to violate his rules. He picked up his pace. As he grabbed the door handle, his other hand was already curled into a fist. Girls needed to be kept in line, lest they become wanton. And no girls under his roof were going to go down that road. He grabbed the staff he kept by the front door. It was only as wide as his thumb, just like the Bible required.

Tituba flew out of the parlor. Her dark skin was slick with perspiration, her hands moving agitatedly. Her Caribbean accent was still pronounced, even though she had been taken from her homeland as a child. "Reverend, thank goodness. Come quick! Come quick!"

Normally such an outburst would earn her a censure, but there was something about her words tonight. He quickly followed her into the parlor. His nine-year-old daughter Betty sat on the couch staring straight ahead. Her eleven-year-old cousin Abigail Williams sat next to her. Neither moved. Neither stirred.

He stopped still with a frown. "What happened?"

"I do not know, master. They came downstairs. Said they could not sleep. I went to get them milk. When I came back I found them like this. I cannot get them to speak to me."

"Betty! Abigail! Look at me!" Neither girl moved.

He reached down and shook Betty. She jerked away from him and slid to the floor, where she began to shake. Abigail slid next to her, also shaking. Then the screams began.

Tituba backed away, her hands in front of her. "The Devil is in them."

The reverend backed away as well, making the sign of the cross. He stared at his daughter and niece as they shook, drool dripping from their mouths. The girls continued to scream, their bodies contorting in unnatural shapes.

"What should we do for them, sir? How do we stop it?" Tituba asked.

But while Tituba's words became more panicked, a calm settled over Samuel. *This* was why he had been sent to Salem. God had known what He was doing, as He always did. He had wanted His soldier Samuel here for this moment. This evil had made a mistake coming to his home.

Tituba grabbed his arm. "Sir, what should we do?"

Samuel shrugged her off, wiping his arm as if to remove the stain of her offending touch. "We will do nothing. But *I* will find the Devil hiding in Salem."

And then Samuel smiled, for now his purpose here was clear.

CHAPTER 6

It had been difficult for each of the sisters to get away, but they had all managed. Now Sarah looked around at the group. Susan Osbourne, Rebecca Nurse, Mary Eastly, Elizabeth Proctor, Martha Carrier, Martha Cory, and their youngest member, Meg Jacobs.

In the streets, each would turn up their nose at Sarah Goode, her role as little more than a town beggar demanding it. But here, here the true nature of her role in this world was respected. Each woman looked to Sarah with unquestioning faith and love. She was their leader and had been these last ten years.

Sarah had led celebrations but also their education. Learning for women was strictly forbidden in Salem, but for the Followers, it was a requirement. Some had been able to hide their skills well, like Martha Cory, who was a shining example of Puritan femininity. But others, such as Sarah, struggled with the submissive role she was forced to play.

But here, with one another, they could be themselves. Sarah's gaze shifted to Meg. Her large hazel eyes dominated her pale face. Her brown hair was tucked away in her bonnet. There was an air of frailness around her which helped her in the Puritan community but which secretly worried Sarah. The time heading towards them would be difficult, but she feared it would be most difficult for Meg. She was quiet, taking after her father rather than her independent mother and grandmother. A great deal would be asked of her. Sarah prayed she was up to the task.

Sarah stood by the fire, and despite the danger she knew was coming, the weight on her shoulders lessening slightly at the sight of her true family. "Good morrow, sisters."

"Good morrow, Sister Sarah," they replied in unison.

Meg met her gaze and Sarah gave her a small smile. "How are you this evening, Meg?"

"I am well, Sister."

"And your grandfather?"

"His arthritis still pains him, but the remedy you gave him eases it. Thank you."

Sarah nodded. The arts of healing had been handed down from sister to sister. The Great Mother had been a great healer as well, sharing her skills to all who needed it. But in this time, they could only share the skills amongst themselves lest others question how they had gained their knowledge. But only occasionally they aided those outside the sisterhood when it could be done quietly. And besides Meg's grandfather was all she had left now. Easing his pain eased Meg's as well, which made the risk well worth it as far as Sarah was concerned. "I'm glad. I have made some more for you to take with you tonight."

"Thank you, Sister."

Sarah nodded, turning her attention back to the whole group. She knew the faces in front of her as well as her own. She knew their hopes, fears, loves and dreams. But now Sarah's own visions overshadowed all of that. Because none of their wants mattered at this moment. At this moment, the Great Mother could be lost to history unless they took steps. Steeling herself for what she needed to say, she began.

"My sisters, as followers of the Great Mother, we know the

world can be a cruel place. We know that women have lost their standing in societies across the globe. We are little more than the bearers of children and the keepers of the hearth. But our heritage shows how we are more than that. We are the beacons of the future. The keeper of the Great Mother's legacy."

She met Rebecca and Mary's gaze, and they each nodded at her, their hands clasped. Strengthened by the faith in their gaze, she straightened her shoulders. "A darkness is coming and bringing with it an old foe."

There was a gasp across the room but no one asked who the foe was. They all knew. Each member was told the true history of the Fallen angels in this world. They knew of their strengths and skills, as well as how they would live their lives over and over again. Fighting the Fallen was never an option, at least not physically. No the only way to truly fight them was mentally. They could not be outrun but they could be outsmarted.

Martha Cory frowned, her delicate pert nose turning up with the action.

"What do they want?"

"The book," Sarah said.

The silence was deafening and then voices rang out all at once.

"It's not possible."

"How do they know?"

"But it is safe."

Rebecca stood up. "Sisters, sisters, let Sarah finish."

Sarah nodded her thanks suddenly feeling exhausted. She sat down on the bench, her hand on her back. "We have always known there is a great secret with the tome of the Great Mother. I fear it is this secret the Fallen are seeking. It must not fall into their grasp, even when we fall into their grasp."

"What do you mean, Sarah? How will we be caught? The Fallen do not take our kind. They kill them," Martha Cory asked.

"That is true. But it is not their strength we need to fear this time. I cannot see exactly what they have planned, but it will be dangerous for all of us." She paused, taking a breath as her stomach rolled. She wasn't sure if it was due to the babe or the topic. "But we must move forward. We must make preparations to preserve the Mother's legacy in case we do not survive."

Elizabeth gasped. "Surely it won't come to that."

"Not all of us will survive this." Sarah hesitated, not sure if she should reveal the truth, but deciding they had a right to know. "I'm not sure any of us will. And we must prepare."

Shock splashed across each of the faces of the woman. More than one hand flew to a mouth. Other hands reached for the hand of the one next to them. Even in their terror, they leaned to one another for strength. Sarah gave them a moment for the revelation to sink in, for the path before them to become clear. One by one, they straightened their backs, their strength returning to their gaze. Even Meg, who still looked terrified, met Sarah's gaze. Sarah had never been so proud of her sisters. Here they stood on the precipice of their worst fears, and yet no one ran. No one asked for a way out. And in that moment, Sarah desperately wanted to find a way to spare these women what was to come. They deserved so much better than what this world had offered them. And so much more than what it was about to deal them.

But that is not in my power. And that is not the plan for us. Great Mother, please give us the strength to face what is to come.

"So what do we do?" Beth Proctor asked.

"We continue as we have. Live your lives. Love your children. Obey your husbands. None of that must change. Do nothing to draw attention to yourselves." Sarah knew they did not need that warning. Their lives had been spent in hiding. They knew how to follow the rules. "But there is one step that must be taken if the worst occurs. If we begin to fall—" She took a breath. "The last of us must hide the book."

The woman began to speak all it once. "We cannot move it."

"We have kept it hidden for good reason."

"It is already hidden."

"Sister, we cannot—"

Sarah put up a hand and they fell quiet once again. "That is only if the worst happens. The Great Mother's legacy must be protected. It is our duty. The world will need her if it is to move out of this time of shadow."

"You said the last is to move it, but move it where?" Rebecca asked. "And for who? If there are none of us left, who will carry on?"

"We have to believe that there are other Followers hidden away in the world as we are. And one day, someone will come looking. That I am sure of."

"Where will we hide it, though?" Martha Cory asked.

"Somewhere no one will ever think to look for it, except for one of the Followers," Rebecca said.

"Where?" Martha Cory asked.

"With the one of us who falls first," Sarah said quietly.

A gasp spread across the room. Meg's voice burst. "But perhaps what you've seen doesn't have to come to pass. Perhaps if we hold our tongues, keep our heads down—"

"We *cannot* avoid what is to come." Sarah smiled at Meg, trying to soften the harshness of her words. Sarah had always thought of Meg as a daughter and had not tried to toughen her to the uglier sides of life. They all had, taking strength in the innocence and purity of their youngest member. Now Sarah worried that kindness had been selfish. It had given the sisters joy to protect her, but she feared it had not prepared Meg for what was to come. But there was no changing it now.

"Even if we were pillars of the community, as many of you already are, the future will still come. Besides, I have never fit in. Knowing who I have been before this life has made the restrictions of this life unbearable. And I cannot and will not hide who I am. I will not pretend to be meek and simpleminded to make those who are meek and simpleminded feel better, especially not with my last days."

Rebecca laid a hand on her shoulder. "But you set a target on your back."

Sarah reached up and grasped it. "That target was placed there a long time ago. And we know that it is not this life that matters, but the next."

"And our children?" Mary asked.

"We prepare them the best we can. There can be no other way." Sarah took a deep breath. "Now I need each of you to swear that you will protect the book, protect the Great Mother's legacy and the knowledge she brings at all costs."

Each of the sisters looked around, their eyes wide. Then Rebecca stood. "For the Great Mother, I swear."

Mary stood next to her. "For the Great Mother, I swear."

Then, one by one, each of the women stood, giving their pledge, ending with Meg, whose voice could barely be heard.

Sarah nodded. "Thank you, Sisters. And may the Great Mother look over us." She smiled, although inside her heart was breaking. For she knew it would not be long until all of these women were wiped from the world's history.

Please give us the strength to face what is to come.

CHAPTER 7

Betty and Abigail had finally snapped out of their states after twenty minutes, but they had not been capable of speaking. Samuel carried them to bed, leaving Tituba with instructions to stay by their side and contact him as soon as they woke up.

Then he'd left for the church. He had an office in the back and made his way there. He went to his small bookshelf. He did not put much stock in reading. People who lost themselves in books were slothful as far as he was concerned, so all the titles here were relevant for his calling. He scanned the titles and pulled out *Memorable Providences Relating to Witchcrafts and Possessions* by Cotton Mather.

Settling behind his desk, he began to read.

It was hours later when he looked up. Mather had detailed the 1688 possession of four children from the Goodwin family by a neighbor, Goody Glover. The children would at times be struck deaf, dumb, and mute all at once. Their limbs would contort to impossible angles, and they would cry out as if being attacked. When Goody Glover, who was an immigrant from Ireland, was taken into custody, the children's afflictions lessened. Glover was found guilty of witchcraft and hung. But the children continued to suffer. Cotton took the eldest daughter into his home to study and help. She would at times bark, purr, and even levitate, but finally prayer and fasting caused the symptoms to subside within a year.

Samuel leaned back, thinking. He knew the Devil was a terrible force in this world. It looked for weakness and struck when people did not guard against it. It was that very weakness that had pushed the Puritans to break away from the Church of England, which had become so lax in its adherence of God's word. And like those early Puritan leaders, Samuel knew that strict adherence to God's word was the only way to salvation.

But someone in my flock has weakened. Someone opened a door and the Devil has slithered in.

He pictured the unnatural state he had found his daughter and niece in. But he knew they were not to blame. No, they were innocents in this. Victims.

He glanced back at the book on his desk. Mather had discovered that the Devil could possess one person, who could then cause fits in another.

That was the only explanation for Betty and Abigail's behavior. They were being assaulted. Someone else, some witch, was tormenting them. And he, as a soldier of Christ, would be the one to find them and cast them out.

He quickly pulled over a sheet of paper. First he needed to get some guidance. He took a breath, composing his thoughts, and then began to write.

To the most learned Mister Mathers . . .

CHAPTER 8

Samuel had sent the letter two days ago and received no response. He knew that distance was part of the culprit. But what if Mr. Mathers did not respond? What if he did not recognize the importance of what was happening here?

I should have stressed my daughter's purity more. Explained why this was not who they were.

He paced along the middle of his parlor. He'd barely been home since the first attack. He'd spent his time re-reading Mather's book and praying for God to aid him.

He went home for a few hours each day. Right after the incident, the girls had slept for hours. When they'd awoken, they had no recollection of what had transpired, but both had dark circles under their eyes.

Since then, they had had two more attacks, the last one this morning when he went home for breakfast. By good fortune, William Griggs, the town physician, was back in town. He had been out of town the last two days tending to an expectant woman. The girls had screamed and contorted. He'd sent for his houseman to fetch Dr. Griggs right away.

The sound of footfalls on the staircase drew Samuel from the parlor. Griggs walked slowly down the stairs, pulling off his glasses and wiping them on his handkerchief.

"Well?" Samuel demanded.

Griggs shook his head as he placed the glasses back on with a shaky hand. "It is not good, Reverend."

"I know that. But what is wrong with them?"

Griggs eyed him steadily. "I think you know. This is beyond my skills as a healer. It is your skills as a preacher that are needed now."

Samuel stepped back, his hand going to his throat. "I had hoped I was wrong."

"You weren't. And whatever you do, do it quickly. Their bodies will not withstand this kind of torment for long." Griggs picked up his coat, which had been slung over the end of the bannister. "I have given them something that should make them sleep, but I cannot guarantee they will not awaken, not if they are attacked again."

"Yes, yes, of course," Samuel murmured, already focused on his next steps as he opened the front door.

"Good day to you, Reverend."

"And you as well," Samuel said, closing the door behind the doctor.

Tituba hurried down the steps toward him. "They are sleeping, Reverend."

"Good." He pulled his hat from the coat stand and placed it on his head. "I will be at the church. Send for me when they awaken." He didn't wait for a reply and hurried from the house.

Keeping his head down, he made his way to the church and stepped into its silent space. The rafters stood twenty feet above his head. The wooden pews were lined up, waiting for the congregants. Samuel had always felt the rightness of his calling when he stepped inside this room. A strength always seemed to seep into his bones, making him walk taller.

But today he only felt cold as he slipped into the last pew. He sat without moving, images from the last few days crowding his mind. He had not been happy when his wife had 'gifted' him with a girl. Now, a son, a son could continue on a legacy, a name. A girl was work and toil. And now, now she was possessed. For a moment, doubt crowded in, asking if he had not done enough to keep her safe.

But he knew that wasn't true. He had provided for her spiritual and physical needs. And when she disobeyed, he brought the wrath of God down upon her. She was an obedient girl. No, someone had targeted her. Someone who probably could not get to him. After all, he was the reverend of Salem, the bulwark against the forces of evil. If someone thought they could reduce his strength by targeting Betty, well, they did not truly understand the depth of his conviction. He knelt and began to pray. He stayed on his knees for an hour, giving thanks to God and asking for guidance in these troubling times.

When he sat back on the pew, his knees and back ached, but his spirit was restored. He was God's soldier and he would not fail in his duty. The door behind him opened and young Dudley Bradstreet poked his head in. "Reverend, good. You have a letter." He quickly walked over to Samuel and handed it over.

Samuel opened it quickly and scanned the contents. Then he smiled. *Yes.*

"Good news, Reverend?"

"Good direction," Samuel corrected him. "I need you to go fetch Thomas Putnam and Dr. Griggs. Tell them I will need their assistance at my home in one hour's time."

"Yes, sir." Dudley quickly left the church.

Samuel looked around, his strength returning. Mather had given him excellent advice, which he would follow to the letter. And soon this scourge would leave his town.

Mather had spoken on the reverend's behalf with the governor, who agreed to convene a court. Two magistrates were already on the way. If all went well, they should arrive today.

Samuel spent the next thirty minutes reviewing Mather's letter and preparing himself for the task ahead before he began the walk back to his home. He knew this was perhaps the most important walk of his life—the walk that would lead to the first battle in this fight.

Thomas Putnam caught up with the reverend as he turned onto his street.

Samuel looked at him in surprise. "Thomas. I was expecting you later."

Thomas was strong large man who owned a large property which he managed extremely well and always donated to the church each week without fail. The reverend had sent for him because he was held in high regard by all in town. And the reverend knew his word and testimony would go a long way in helping the people of Salem truly grasp the danger they were in.

Thomas bowed his head slightly toward the reverend in a show of respect. "I heard your daughters were ill. Ann insisted on going to see them to cheer them up."

Samuels's gaze whipped to Thomas. "Your daughter is at my house?"

"Yes, I stopped there with her on my way into town."

"We must hurry." Samuel began to run.

Holding on to his hat, Thomas ran next to him. "What is it? What is wrong?"

"My daughters are not ill. They have been possessed. There is witchcraft afoot in Salem."

Thomas stumbled, and then with a roar, sprinted past Samuel. He bolted up the path and threw open the door to Samuel's home. "Ann!"

Samuel caught up with Thomas as he was stepping from the parlor and heading for the stairs.

"Father, what is it?" Ann Putnam, age eleven, stood at the top of the staircase. Her large blue eyes looked down at her father with concern before shifting to Samuel. "Reverend."

Samuel was struck yet again by the beauty of the child. With her long, pale blonde hair, she always appeared as he thought angels would.

Thomas rushed up the stairs and grabbed Ann's hand. "You must leave."

"Father, you are hurting me!"

Thomas lessened his grip but kept pulling Ann to the stairs. "It is not safe. You must go."

"What is not safe?"

"You must go home right away. Speak to no one. Directly home, do you understand?"

"Yes, Father," Ann answered, a tremor in her voice.

"Now go." Thomas pushed her toward the door. With a confused look at her father, Ann left just as Dr. Griggs appeared at the end of the path.

Samuel watched her greet the doctor and head down the street. She seemed fine but she would have to be watched carefully.

Dr. Griggs closed the door after entering. Samuel directed his attention to the two men dismissing Ann Putnam from his thoughts. "We must question my niece and daughter. They will tell us who has afflicted them."

"But the Devil will trick them. How will they know?"

Samuel held up the letter from Mather. "I have consulted an expert. He has told me what to do, what to say. We will get the answers. But it will not be easy. You must prepare yourselves."

Thomas looked at him and nodded. Griggs did the same. Samuel picked up the rod from next to the door and headed up the stairs. "We go into battle, men."

CHAPTER 9

Her hand on her lower back, Sarah Goode lowered herself to the stool. The babe's position caused pain to radiate through her. All day she had struggled with it. She was only a few months along and already this was proving to be the most difficult pregnancy.

"Mama, do you need some water?" her five-year old daughter Dorcas asked quietly, the large eyes that were identical to Sarah's staring at her with hope that she could help.

Sarah smiled. Dorcas was a smaller version of herself, with her large eyes and light brown hair. But beyond the physical resemblance, they were like night and day. Sarah did not think she had ever been so kind, or so patient. She was sure she had been cynical from the day she was born. But Dorcas lived in a glow of light that touched all who met her. She was a gift, one Sarah would be forever thankful for. Sarah ran a hand through her daughter's hair, pulling her gently forward to kiss her forehead. "All I need is one of your healing hugs."

Dorcas smiled and wrapped her arms around Sarah. Dorcas was her spot of joy in this difficult world. Sweet, considerate, with a shy smile, she was everything that was right with this world. She gave Sarah strength. With a sigh, Sarah leaned her head on her daughter. It was these moments that made life worthwhile. Sarah had three other children, all boys. She loved them, but there was something about Dorcas that wrapped around her heart and tugged.

Dorcas put a hand on her mother's belly. "Is my sister giving you pain?"

"No, dearie, she is wonderful, just as you are."

Dorcas had told Sarah a month ago that she was having a girl. Sarah wasn't sure if it was wishful thinking or if Dorcas too might have the gift. She hoped it was the former. She did not want Dorcas burdened with the sight, especially not at such a young age.

A sharp rap on the door broke into the peaceful moment, and Sarah's head jerked up as a voice boomed out. "In the name of the Court of Oyer, I demand this door be opened."

Sarah's heart pounded. Dorcas grasped her hand. "Mama?"

Sarah ran a trembling hand through her daughter's hair. *I'm not ready*. But she steeled herself, facing her daughter. She kissed each of her cheeks. "Always remember you are loved and that you are important. Promise me."

"I promise, Mama."

Sarah nodded. "Now go, hide in your room. Do not come out until it is silent."

Dorcas's eyes grew larger and her bottom lip trembled. "Mama?"

"Go, Dorcas." Then she softened her tone. "Go."

With one last look, Dorcas fled for her room. Bracing herself, Sarah hoisted herself from the stool, one hand on her on her lower back as she made her way to the front door. The knock sounded again, louder this time. "I demand you open this door."

Closing her eyes, she prayed for strength before unlatching the door and swinging it open. A man she had never seen before stood there. He was tall and stout, with gray hair that reached his shoulders but a young face. Behind him was Reverend Samuel, his Bible clasped in his hands. He made the sign of the cross. Thomas Putnam stood with Samuel, along with three other men from town.

"Sarah Goode, you have been charged with the crime of witchcraft." The man wrapped his hand around her upper arm and pulled her from the house.

Sarah stumbled. But the man didn't slow. Sarah bit her lip trying to keep the angry response from her lips. If Dorcas heard her, she would come out to see, and Sarah would not have her exposed to this lunacy.

Thomas narrowed his eyes as she passed and then spit on her. Sarah didn't have time to wipe it off as she was unceremoniously pulled down the street. Her neighbors stood watching her go by, many turning their backs. But Sarah got her balance, held her chin high, and straightened her back.

It begins.

CHAPTER 10

The cold that had begun to seep into Sarah's bones on the walk from her home to the courthouse had not abated. They had stripped her when she'd arrived, looking for the mark of the witch. There had been none to find, of course, but that had not convinced them of her innocence. She had been thrown in a cell without even a question asked.

"Sarah!" Susan Osbourne rushed to her as the cell slammed shut. "They got you, too?"

"Just before they picked you up."

"What is going on? Why do they think we are witches?"

"We have been accused of attacking Betty Samuel and Abigail Williams."

"I've never even spoken to those girls, never mind laid a finger on them."

"They say our specters attacked them."

Sarah stared at her in disbelief. "That's preposterous. If I had that ability I assure you I would haunt my husband to get him to work harder."

Susan shook her head. "It's ridiculous, I agree. But Reverend

Samuel claims with the spectral evidence, they have more than enough to hang us."

Sarah felt light-headed, even though she had known her death was coming.

"So this is how it will end," she said softly.

Susan helped Sarah over to the cot. "You saw this, did you not?"

"Not the form it would take. Only that we were all in danger. If I had known they were coming for you, I would have warned you."

Susan placed her hand on Sarah's arm. "I know, Sister."

Sarah squeezed her arm back and Susan winced. "What is wrong?"

"Nothing. My bones are just aching a bit today. And I did not have a chance to take my medicine."

Sarah studied her friend closely. Susan looked pale, and there was a sheen of sweat on her forehead. She had been ill for years, rarely leaving her house, although she faithfully met with her sisters.

Susan patted her arm. "Do not look at me like that. I will be fine. And even if I am not, there is nothing we can do about it in here anyway."

"So what *can* we do?"

Susan shook her head. "Surely they will not convict us, just on the visitations from two girls?"

"No, no, of course not. And no one else will step forward. No one could."

A shriek tore through the hall and Sarah gasped.

"What on earth is that?" Susan asked, her hand at her throat and her eyes wide.

Sarah hurried to the bars and peered through as three people appeared at the end of the hall. Two men had Tituba by the arms and pulled her roughly along.

Tituba screamed and cried, saying words in a language that Sarah Goode did not recognize.

Sarah and Susan exchanged a look. Tituba's ramblings continued unabated as she was locked away. If anyone was looking for a witch, Tituba's violent ramblings would surely convince them.

Reverend Samuel appeared at the cell door, and both Sarah and Susan jumped back. His approach had been undetected due to Tituba's screams.

Samuel's eyes bored into Sarah's. "It's time we had a chat." He nodded to the two men who had escorted Tituba. "Take her."

Blessed Mother, give me strength. Sarah repeated the phrase to herself over as she was pulled from the cell and led from to the Reverend's office at the back of the church.

Two men waited for them there. Neither was from Salem and both frowned as they inspected Sarah from head to foot.

The two men who escorted her pushed her into the middle of the room. Sarah whirled around and glared at them but neither looked at her.

"Leave us," one of the ones she did not know said. With a bow to the men, they stepped out of the room.

Sarah turned to the men. "Are you two the ones behind this farce? Are you my accusers?"

One of the men stepped forward. "How dare you, witch. I am Jonathan Corwin, sworn magistrate of the court."

"And I am Magistrate John Hathorne. We will prosecute your case, such that it is. The evidence is substantial. You should plead guilty and beg the court for mercy."

Their arrogance and condescension tripped her emotions from fear to anger. She laughed looking down her nose at the men. "Evidence? There is no evidence, for I am not a witch. What *evidence* do you have of my alleged crime?"

"We have three who have borne witness against you."

Sarah frowned. Witnesses? "Who?"

"That is not—"

"Who?" Sarah demanded.

Jonathan narrowed his eyes, his mouth a tight line. "Ann Putnam, Abigail Williams, and Elizabeth Samuel."

Sarah laughed. "Children? You dragged me in here on the word of children? Children lie, Magistrate."

Samuel bounded from his chair. "How dare you. My daughter and niece would never lie. They are God-fearing children."

Sarah shook her head. Obviously the man had never spent much time around children if he believed that argument. "All children lie. It is part of their nature."

"And Tituba? Why would *she* lie?" Hathorne asked.

Sarah frowned. Seeing Tituba dragged down the hall again in her mind, she turned to Samuel. "Tituba? *Your* slave? She would lie because you told her to."

Samuel slapped Sarah across the face. "You accuse me of laying false claims to the court, witch?"

Sarah's hand flew to the side of her face. Her cheek throbbed and tears sprang to her eyes. But they were not tears of fear. Oh no, these were tears of anger.

"I know you are a witch. I know you torment my child even now. And your evil has stained the good people of Salem. You have never fit in because the people of Salem know your true nature. Admit to who you are."

"I am Sarah Goode. And that is all that I am."

"Liar! The devil acts through you. And the devil will rue the day he came for my daughter." Samuel questioned her fast and furious, barely giving her time to respond and never letting her complete an answer. Finally, she gave up. This man would not listen. He had decided who she was, what she was and there was nothing she could say or do that would change that.

"Answer me!" Samuel screamed, his face red as he stepped toward Sarah again his hand held high.

Hathorne grabbed his arm before he could make contact.

"Now, now there is no need for that." He moved to stand in front of Sarah, shooing Samuel away. Sarah glared at Samuel and he seethed right back at her. *That man is insane.*

"Sister Goode," Hathorne said pulling her attention back to him. Until Hathorne had intervened, Sarah had forgotten the other two were in the room. They'd seemed content to let Samuel run the show.

Now Hathorne smiled at her although there was no warmth in it. "Surely you trust in the goodness of God? He has provided us this blessed world as a gift and we have been entreated to dole out justice on his behalf. That justice extends to even you. Now tell us what you have done and see the justice this world can provide."

Sarah shook her head, choking down a laugh at the absurdity of his statement. "You speak of justice, you men who own your wives and daughters as if they were slaves. This world married me off to one man, who spent all my money and left me in debt and then married me off to a second who has barely worked a full day in his life. That is what the world has provided me. And I am sick of going along with it. I've seen the *justice* of this world and it is anything but just."

Corwin glared at her. "If you continue this way, you will be hanged."

She looked into Corwin's face. "Do you honestly think that I am stupid enough to believe that there is any way I am going to avoid that fate? If I am going to hang, I will damn well do it as I am, not as the person you want me to be. I am innocent."

The pretense of civility dropped from Hathorne's face. "You are not! Now admit your sins."

She looked at the men in front of her. There was nothing she would be able to say to convince them either, so she resolved to stay silent. Her words were meaningless anyway.

They continued to question her for another hour, but Sarah stayed silent. Finally, Corwin threw up his hands. "We leave her in your hands, Reverend Samuel. We will return after supper."

Samuel inclined his head. "As you wish, Magistrates."

Samuel was silent as the magistrates left but as soon as the door closed he turned and began to circle Sarah. But Sarah just ignored him. She had no interest in the questions of this little man. The three of them had offered her freedom in exchange for her turning in the other 'members' of her coven. Apparently they could stomach a witch amongst them so long as she was a disloyal witch. They made her sick.

Samuel walked over to the table and poured himself a drink of water. Sarah had not had a drop the entire time she had been held and her mouth was so dry. She looked at the glass longingly.

Samuel finished his drink and sighed. "Ah. Now, where were we? Ah, yes, you were about to tell me the names of the others in your coven."

Sarah said nothing, just stared at a spot on the wall as he continued to ramble. She fought the weariness falling over her, but then she closed her eyes. She was so tired she was swaying on her feet. A hard pinch on her arm caused her eyes to fly open with a gasp.

"Pay attention, witch."

"For the last time, I am not a witch, you stupid man."

Samuel glared at her. "You are a woman who does not know her place. You attacked my child, my niece—two innocents."

"Why on earth would I have done that?" Sarah asked, feeling beyond exasperate.

"Perhaps they stumbled upon something they shouldn't have. Perhaps they found your book."

Sarah's head whipped up and her eyes went wide before she could even think to hide her reaction.

"Ah, I see have your attention now." He smiled. "Where are your smart retorts now, witch? I know you have a book of spells."

Her heart raced and it was only sheer willpower that kept her on her feet.

"Tell me where the book is or your daughter will tell us I'm sure. Dorcas is her name, isn't it?"

Fear slashed through Sarah. Not Dorcas. "Leave her alone." She wanted the words to come out as a command but they shook too much to have any authority in them.

Samuel's tone hardened. "Tell me where it is."

The vision enveloped her before she could respond and Samuel disappeared. Instead she found herself in a castle in a distant land. Samuel was there demanding attention from a woman with blonde hair and incredibly blue eyes.

"I want you, Helen."

The woman's face displayed her disgust as she raked him with her eyes. "Lay a finger on me and I will make you a eunuch."

Samuel's face grew red. "If I say—"

"What do you want, Samuel? Because if it is to bed me, I assure you, you will not enjoy the encounter."

The vision disappeared as quickly as it appeared and she quickly realized he had not noticed her slip in and out of the vision. And by some miracle, she had remained standing.

She also realized something else in that moment: the souls of the two men were the same; only their faces differed. He was the same throughout time: a small man demanding people acknowledge his importance. And until he got beyond his own ego, he would spend all his lifetimes trying to reach the same impossible goal.

The woman ignored his demands, and across time, Sarah felt her resolve. It strengthened her.

Samuel stopped his pacing and turned to her. "Tell me where your grimoire is."

You small little man. She shook her head. "There is nothing to tell. I am not a witch and I have no grimoire."

"Then I will ask your daughter. Would you like that?"

Sarah stared at him, feeling her helplessness. But that state of helplessness was one that, as a woman, she was used to. Her first husband had doomed her children to a life of poverty. Her gender had doomed her to machinations of all men. And she knew right now that no matter what she did, she would not be able to spare her daughter from the same fate.

But if she told them, the lessons of the Great Mother would be lost for all time. The mission of the Great Mother, to bring the world to a place of compassion, truth, and justice would never be realized. And once again, it would be women who would bear the cost of that future world.

But she also knew there was an important secret within the pages of the Great Mother's tome. And whatever that secret was would be the tipping point in the fight between good and evil. This world had designated her powerless at birth. But she still had power in the greater fight. And she would not hand it over to this little man, not even as her heart broke at the thought of Dorcas being in their clutches.

"I won't tell you anything."

"Then you doom her to your fate."

Sarah's throat clogged with emotion, and tears pressed against the back of her eyes. Her silence was her only power. She knew this world was not the important one. This was the schoolroom where people learned the lessons needed to move on to the next. If they did not learn those lessons they were doomed to return over and over. And as she looked at Samuel, she knew he was doomed. His soul would never reach peace.

"She has chosen her own fate." And as Sarah said the words, she felt their truth. *Before we entered this world, we chose the obstacles we would face.* Her daughter, her brave, beautiful girl, would suffer. But only in this life, and then she would move on. And she would be free, unlike this man in front of her.

Growling, Samuel stormed over to the door and flung it open. "Take her away. And bring me her daughter."

The men who'd escorted her earlier grabbed her roughly by the arms and Sarah closed her eyes. *I'm sorry, my child. If I could take your place, I would.*

CHAPTER 11

The town went wild with talk as soon as the arrests had been made. Puritans did not show excitement. They eschewed public displays and gossip was severely frowned upon. But the arrest of three women for witchcraft was simply too scintillating for people to remain quiet. Meg's grandfather had insisted she stay out of town until the hysteria died down. It had been three weeks now, and she had heard little to nothing about the trials. But she had learned that today was Susan's trial, and Meg had convinced him to come.

As Meg and her grandfather made their way into town, they'd been informed that Tituba had fingered both Sarah Goode and Susan Osbourne as witches, corroborating the accusations of the girls.

"This is insanity," her grandfather growled. "Those women are no more witches than you are."

Meg nodded, fear clogging her throat. When she had learned of Sarah and Susan's arrest, she had been stunned-stunned and terrified. When Sarah had warned them, Meg had managed to convince herself that Sarah's vision was only a possible future, not a guarantee. In fact, she had convinced herself that if she was extra good, she could help avoid the whole catastrophe. But yet again, the world had shown her how useless her actions were in preventing harm. Meg was not one who controlled destiny or fate. She was merely a rudderless ship being pushed along by its whims.

Ahead, Rebecca Nurse's white hair shone in the sunlight as she stood outside the church, clutching the sleeve of her son, Benjamin. Rebecca was seventy-one this year. And Meg had always thought she looked much younger, her energy and vitality giving her a youthfulness. But today, she looked her age as she held onto her son. Meg nodded toward her. "There is Rebecca. I will go speak with her."

"Yes, yes, go ahead." Her grandfather turned to speak with a group of men.

Meg hurried across the road and Rebecca turned, her eyes red and filled with tears. "Rebecca? What has happened?"

Rebecca patted her son's arm. "Will you give us a moment, Benjamin?"

"Of course, Mother." He nodded at Meg as he took his leave.

"What is it?" Meg asked. Her anxiety grew as Rebecca stayed silent.

"It is Susan Osborne," she said softly.

"The trial? But she hasn't even—"

"There will be no trial for Susan. She died last night."

Meg felt her world tilt. Susan had been the sister who had exposed her to the Greek myths and taught her to see beyond the history written by men, for men. "How?"

"Her husband tried to get her medicine to her. But he could not afford the medicine *and* the cost of food. He had to choose."

Meg closed her eyes, imagining Susan's suffering. One of the cruelest aspects of prison was that inmates had to pay for their food, their beds, medicine, everything. And those that could not did not survive for long.

Rebecca looked toward the prison, a tremor in her voice.

"Sarah Goode was with her when she passed. That is one saving grace."

Meg nodded, not able to speak for a moment overcome with senselessness of Susan's death. What purpose did it serve? What purpose did any of this serve? Images of Susan and her quiet ways filled Meg's mind and hole opened up in her chest. *Oh Susan, you did not deserve this.* "And the trial for Sarah? Will it still go forward?"

"Yes. And they have arrested someone else."

"Who?"

"Bridget Bishop."

Meg frowned. "Bridget?" She was not one of the followers.

"If Sarah is found guilty, they will not hang her right away. She is pregnant. They will allow her to give birth. But I feel the people in this town want to see a witch hang. And Bridget is easy enough to hate."

Meg knew Rebecca was right. All anyone had been able to speak about these last few weeks was the evil of witches and the need to cleanse this town. The righteous anger of the town was a palpable thing and she knew they wanted to act. Susan's death would not allow them that. Tituba was a slave and viewed as a pawn. No, people wanted to strike back. And Bridget, while she was not a sister, but she was not like the other women of Salem. She had been seen flirting with men in the town and was believed to have even slept with some of the men outside the marriage bed. She was a good target for the town's rage.

Meg closed her eyes, feeling the powerlessness of the moment. "What is happening?"

"They say they are trying to root out evil. But all I see is the evil they are perpetrating." Rebecca paused. "There is one more piece of news. You must prepare yourself."

"What could be worse than this?"

"They have arrested Dorcas."

Meg's mind went blank for a moment, trying to figure out

who Rebecca could be speaking of. She only knew one person by that name, and they couldn't possibly... "She's only five years old."

Rebecca nodded. "I believe they are trying to get Sarah to confess by threatening Dorcas."

"Will she?"

Rebecca shook her head slowly. "No. Sarah knows what is at stake goes beyond even one life. And that each of us chose the crosses we would bear before we arrived in this world. Even Dorcas."

Meg knew her words were right, but she still felt the ugliness, the cruelness of the moment. Dorcas was a child. She should not have to be exposed to this. "What will we do?"

"There is nothing we can do. We see this through to the end. We protect the legacy. We prepare the way for those coming after us."

"But surely there must be something more we can do."

"No, child. This is out of our hands now. It is in God's."

Meg looked at the church as a coffin was carried out. *Susan.* Her heart seemed to stumble and her chest felt heavy as she glanced away from the coffin and toward the sky. *Dear God, why are you doing this to your Followers?*

Rebecca squeezed her arm gently, which was as much affection as she dared show. "Now clear your eyes, child. And go to your Grandfather. He awaits you."

Meg nodded, taking a breath. "Be careful, Rebecca."

Rebecca gazed for a long moment into Meg's eye. "You as well, child." She slowly headed toward her son.

Meg turned to find her grandfather. She caught sight of him through the crowd and headed toward him. She skirted around a group of young men, keeping her gaze on the ground. *This cannot be happening.* Her gaze still cast downward, she jumped back as two feet appeared in her view. Hand to her chest, Meg stepped back quickly, her hand to her throat as she stared at Ann Putnam. "Ann, I did not hear you approach."

"I am quiet these days."

Meg frowned. *What a strange thing to say.*

Ann tilted her head, looking toward the coffin before returning her gaze to Meg. "Terrible thing about Susan, is it not? To die that way? Of course, the rest of their deaths will be no less easy."

Meg's mouth fell open at her tone. It was so unemotional. "Ann, why would you say such a thing?"

She smiled and leaned forward as if to tell Meg a secret. "The Devil told me to say it," she whispered.

Meg reared back.

But Ann just laughed. "The Devil is alive and well in Salem, Meg, and he is looking for something. He won't stop until he finds it. You should remember that."

Meg backed away from her, her whole body shaking. Then Ann let out a shriek and collapsed to the ground. Everyone turned to look, and Thomas Putnam pushed through the crowd.

"She is killing me, Father!" Ann cried out.

"Who? Who is doing it?" Thomas knelt next to her but didn't touch her.

"Sarah Goode!" Ann screamed her name and then dropped away into a faint. The crowd murmured angrily around Meg, but she could only stare at the child on the ground. What was happening?

Meg knew that Sarah was not evil. But Ann's words, her convulsions, they sent a stab of cold right through Meg.

Dear God, what is happening?

CHAPTER 12

Guilty. The word reverberated through Sarah's mind as she was brought back to her cell. They had found her guilty.

Those girls had stood up in court and lied, accusing her of all sorts of vile acts. And no one had doubted them. These people who she had known for years believed her to be a witch. She knew they held no love for her but to want her dead? And for the life of her, Sarah could not figure out how it had come to this. Why Salem? Why now? And how did the reverend know of the book? He'd questioned her again just before trial asking her about the book. Yet she did not think he was a Fallen. He'd given no indication of it, in fact, he didn't really seem to understand what the book contained. But someone had told him.

Sarah had stared at the crowd watching the trial wondering who had gotten to the reverend. but she had no clue. And there had been so many people. People had come in from other towns to see the trials, the news of them travelling far and wide. Even reverends from other villages had come to watch the spectacle. Sarah saw Reverend Nicholas Noyes. She remembered him from her childhood, a cruel, cold man willing to dispense God's judgment with a rod for any indiscretion. These trials reaffirmed everything he believed wrong with the wickedness of the women in the world.

The babe kicked her just as she stepped into the hallway leading to her cell. Sarah grimaced, putting a hand on her belly. One of her guards caught sight of the motion.

"The spawn of the Devil grows there. The judge should have put you both to death."

"But he did not, did he?" No one had been more surprised than Sarah when her execution had been delayed until after the birth of her babe. The judge had decreed that the child could be innocent and he could not in good conscious sentence it to death.

Of course, my other daughter is an innocent as well, but they have no trouble punishing her.

Dorcas remained locked up. Sarah had not seen her the entire time, but she had heard her cries. They had stabbed through her as if they were knives. Her husband had tried to get Dorcas released, but nothing had worked. He had even testified against Sarah in the hopes it would secure Dorcas's freedom.

It had hurt to hear Daniel say those things, but she would take that hurt multiplied by a hundred if it could secure her daughter's release.

The one thing she could not do was give him the book, as much as it killed her. And after her babe was born, that commitment would, in fact, kill her.

Just as it killed Susan. Susan had never made it to trial. She had grown weaker and weaker as time went on. Sarah had shared her food, but still Susan weakened. Sarah had been holding her hand when she died. And she'd lain with Susan in her arms until the guards had taken her body away.

Susan had raged with fever for the last few days, and instead of offering her aid, her captors had taken it as more proof of her guilt.

Last night, Sarah Goode had sat by her side, holding her hard and constantly cooling her brow. Susan was lucid toward the end, and they had talked of the good times and the time when they would see each other again in a better place.

Then she had drifted into sleep and slipped from this world. The ache of her loss hung over Sarah, infesting every cell in her body. But at the same time, she was glad her friend had gone on to a better place. There was nothing but suffering left for them here.

They reached her cell, and the guard unlocked the door and pushed Sarah inside. She stumbled over to the cot and curled up. The babe was quiet now, for which she was thankful. She ran her hand over her belly. *It is not a good world you will enter soon.*

Closing her eyes, she let out a sigh and prayed for the oblivion of sleep. And for once, the world was merciful.

∼

"TIME TO WAKE UP, SARAH."

Blinking awake, it took Sarah awhile to recognize where she was. And when she did, she wanted nothing more than to return to her dream. She and Susan had been walking arm and arm along a brook. Dorcas was ten and jumping from rock to rock with a laugh. Her little sister trailed behind her, copying her moves and taking Dorcas's hand when the distance was too great. It had been peaceful, and beautiful, and false. But Sarah had enjoyed every moment.

"Oh, Sarah," a voice sang at her. The lock turned in the cell door. Sarah sat up awkwardly, her stomach forcing her to push off the wall to get upright.

Ann Putnam stood smiling at her—*inside* her cell.

Sarah got slowly to her feet. "What are you doing here? How did you get into this cell?"

Ann held up a set of keys. "Why, I let myself in."

Sarah frowned as she studied the girl. Something was very wrong here. "Are you all right?"

"Why, I am just great. Thank you for asking. How are you?

Must have been quite a shock to be found guilty when you are not a witch."

Sarah's mouth fell open and she didn't know what to say.

Ann just smiled. "You are, however, a Follower, are you not?"

"Ann, what are you doing? Why are you saying these things?"

Ann tilted her head and smiled.

Sarah narrowed her eyes, a dark thought crowding her mind. "*Who* are you?"

Ann threw back her head and laughed. "Ah, so you figured it out. I was wondering when you would. I kept waiting and waiting. But honestly, it was taking *forever*. So I decided I should come for a little visit." She flounced over to the cot and flopped down, straightening her dress.

Sarah stood still, her eyes rooted on the 'child,' in front of her. "You are too young. You should not know anything yet."

"True. I should not. To be honest, I am not even sure this vessel will ever come into any powers. And yet, here I am." She spread her arms wide.

"Who are you?"

"Names are not important, not really. Just know I am one of the top lieutenants of my great liege. And even now, I do his bidding."

Sarah began to shake and she backed up until her back hit the bars of the cell. "How is this possible?"

"Tituba. What a wonderfully strange woman. Did you know she was kidnapped as a child and sold into slavery?" Ann knocked on her head. "Between you and me, I think it made her a little unstable. But it was actually a blessing, at least for me. Because she spent time with other slaves who were practitioners of the dark arts."

Sarah felt light-headed. "So Tituba *is* a witch."

Ann waved away Sarah's words. "Oh please. There is no such things as witches. No, she does not really know what she is doing. But she does know some of the ceremonies, some of the potions, and she managed to open a door that I slipped right through. Lucky, no?"

Sarah's head was spinning and she gripped the bars behind her to keep from falling. Ann was a Fallen, or at least would be one day. "When did this happen? How did no one know?"

"Well, the girls and I would gather at Reverend Samuel's home and tell stories. He was never around, of course. So we only had Tituba to watch us. And she showed us what she had learned."

"What about Abigail and Elizabeth? Or any of the others? Are they also—"

Ann shook her head. "Just girls."

"But the fits. . ."

Ann smiled. "Also thanks to Tituba. Do you know there are roots that can cause delusions, vomiting, spasms? I sprinkle it into the girls' food whenever I need them to respond."

"But why target us?"

Ann held up her hands, a sheepish smile on her face. "Well, once again, that is my fault. Turns out they *are* easily manipulated. I suppose it is from having a complete donkey for a father. That man would not know a kind word if it bit him on the behind. But the upside of that kind of upbringing is a little praise can make them receptive to any idea."

"Why are you telling me all of this? I could tell them what you have said."

"And why would they believe you? We are merely three innocent girls, victims to the evil deeds of the witches in our midst." She shrugged. "So go ahead. You, a female with no standing, tell all those male judges that I, a child, am the mastermind behind everything. See how far that gets you."

Sarah reeled as the truth stared her in the face. "You did all of this. Why?"

"Oh, you know why. Think *really* hard for a moment."

"You want the book."

Ann clapped. "And a prize for Sarah. Very good. Now, where is it?"

Sarah reeled. This child had set everything into motion. She had targeted all of them. She was responsible for Susan's death. But more importantly, she was doing all of this to gain the knowledge in the book. And she could not have it. Sarah straightened away from the bars. "I will not tell you."

Ann blew out a breath. "You see now, that is a problem, because I *really* do need it."

"It was you. You told them about the book."

There was no point denying its existence. If Ann was truly a Fallen, one of Samyaza's top officers, he would know of the book. And given her surroundings, straight denial seemed pointless.

Ann smiled. "Once again, very good. I did not tell them, exactly, but I did leave hints. You humans—always scrambling after glory. And that Cotton Mathers, well, he scrambles a little more than most."

"But how? No matter who you are inside, you are still a child outside."

"A child with *wonderful* penmanship. A few notes sent his way, pushing him in the right direction, a few clues hinting where to look. And then when the accusations appeared, why, he knew exactly what to do. And how to get the reverend to do it."

"All of this for the book? Why? Why would you care about some ancient book? It has nothing to do with you."

Genuine surprise flashed across Ann's face. And then she laughed and laughed. She held on to her stomach and rolled with mirth. Finally she got ahold of herself and wiped at her eyes. "Oh, God, you don't know. You are all willing to lay down your lives and you have no idea why."

Sarah narrowed her eyes. She knew that within the tome was a weapon that would determine the course of the fight between good and evil. She had been taught the words, but what Ann said was true. She didn't know what the weapon was or how to wield it. She'd read the tome many times, but she'd never seen any mention of a weapon. Part of her worried that perhaps the pages with the weapon had been lost.

But if Ann wanted it then they were right to defend it with their lives.

Ann grinned, shaking her head. "It is just pure dumb loyalty, is it? I will give your Great Mother that. She has always been able to inspire loyalty in her Followers." Ann tapped her finger to her lips. "But what to do now? I thought locking you up here, having your daughter locked up, would do the trick. Maybe I underestimated that maternal bond."

Sarah curled her right hand into a fist while her other covered her protruding belly.

Ann raised an eyebrow. "Or perhaps not. Perhaps I was wrong to focus on emotional pain. You women seem to have a great deal of practice at dealing with that. Perhaps I should have focused more on physical pain."

"Whatever you do, I will *not* tell you."

Ann tilted her head, her lips pursed as she studied Sarah. "Hm, I actually believe you. That *is* a bit of a problem. Because you see, I figured after a few nights in here, faced with the looming specter of death, you would fold. But apparently you have not been properly motivated yet." Ann hopped off the bed. "Well, I will have to see what I can do about that."

Sarah rushed across the room and grabbed Ann's arm. "Whatever you are planning will not work. I will never tell you. None of us will."

Ann looked down at where Sarah's hand was wrapped around her forearm and looked back up at Sarah with a huge smile. Then she opened her mouth and screamed, her smile in place the whole time.

Guards shouted from down the hall. Sarah dropped Ann's arm and stumbled back, but Ann continued to scream. Thomas appeared at the bars and Ann's smile disappeared, her body contorting into an odd shape.

"Get this door open!" Thomas yelled.

Sarah stared at Ann in horror. She was bent to the side, her right shoulder raised, her left dropped by her side. The tilt of her neck was unnatural and her eyes were dead. Yet still she screamed.

"She is attacking her!" Thomas yelled.

"I am not! I have done nothing." Sarah backed away from the bars until her back hit the wall. Thomas rushed into the cell, his eyes afire. Sarah put her hands in front of her as if she could keep him back. Behind him, Ann continued to scream, keeping in her contorted shape, but she winked at Sarah.

"Witch!" Thomas yelled as his fist collided with the side of Sarah's jaw.

Sarah's head whipped to the side, her hand slamming into the wall as she crumpled to the floor.

CHAPTER 13

Three months had passed since Ann's first visit. She had come to visit three more times, always when Sarah was alone. The last time, she ticked off the names of all of the Followers. But that was not where Ann's treachery ended.

The Followers knew of the Fallen, but Sarah had never met one. She thought they might be myths like the Roman and Greek gods, exaggerations of real people. But if anything the tome had undersold the cruelty of the Fallen. In the time Sarah had been locked up, dozens more had been accused. Most named others, who named others, until Sarah had lost track of all the 'witches' roaming Salem. All her sisters, save Meg, had been accused, including Rebecca, whose trial was tomorrow. Rebecca was a woman in good standing, and her arrest had the already shell-shocked town in a full-blown panic. But not enough to rescind the arrest warrant.

Ann had taken great relish in speaking of Rebecca's arrest, so Sarah had no doubt that Rebecca would not be freed through tomorrow's trial. No, she would be damned by it. Sarah looked into Rebecca's concerned face. Rebecca and her sister, Mary, had been like mothers to all the Followers. And selfish as it was, she was glad she had Rebecca with her now.

Sarah squirmed, pains shooting through her midsection. The labor had started earlier in the day but Sarah had said nothing. Rebecca noticed hours ago, as had her sisters, but they'd stayed quiet as well. But now, as the night turned darker, Sarah knew time was growing short. The pain was increasing and the contractions were coming more often.

The baby was not cooperating, and Sarah knew something was wrong.

Rebecca pushed Sarah's hair back. "Are you sure you don't want me to call for help?"

"Even if you did, they would provide none. It is better this way. I want my daughter born surrounded by love, not hate and fear."

Rebecca took her hand, and as Sarah turned to look in her eyes, she was grateful they had been placed in the same cell. "The babe will be here soon."

"Yes." As if her agreement had spurred the babe on, her labor began in earnest. She labored for hours, and still the babe would not come. She fell back heavily into Martha's arms. "Something is wrong."

Rebecca nodded. "I believe the child is facing the wrong direction. I will need to push on your belly to change its position."

Sarah had been thinking the same thing. But before she could say anything, Elisabeth Howe, another woman who shared their cell but was not a Follower, spoke. "But you cannot. If you interfere with the birth—"

Sarah cut her off, grimacing as pain charged through her. "They will try me as a witch? I think we are beyond that worry now."

"Are you ready?" Rebecca asked.

Martha helped prop her up and Sarah nodded. "Yes."

Twenty minutes later, Sarah delivered her little girl. She never cried. She never wiggled. She never breathed. The cord was wrapped around her neck when she entered the world.

Tears flowed down Sarah's cheeks as she cradled her daughter to her chest. She cursed Samuel and the court and the magistrate, blaming them for her daughter's death. Sarah ran her hand over her daughter's face, memorizing each line. She looked so like Dorcas, except she had a more determined chin.

"You look so much like your sister. She wanted to meet you so terribly." A choked sob escaped her and her chest shuddered. All these months she had held back her fear, her horror, knowing she needed to be strong. But as she stared into the face of her lifeless child, all the walls she built up against her emotions crumbled and she felt like she was drowning in a sea of regret, sorrow, and helplessness.

Rebecca sat down gently next to her and pulled both mother and child into her shoulder. Then Sarah sobbed until she had no tears left.

"She is beautiful, Sarah," Martha said, tears in her own eyes.

"What have you named her?" Rebecca asked.

Sarah ran a finger down her daughter's cheek as a tear followed the same path down her own cheek. "Her name is Mercy. For it is a mercy that she was spared the cruelty of this life."

But even as she knew her words were true, she wished she'd had the chance to look in her daughter's eyes just once. She kissed Mercy on the forehead and held her tight as the tears flowed.

You were never meant for this world, little one. And perhaps it is blessing. For the world you would have entered is a cruel one. Better you go on to a loving place.

"The guards come," Rebecca whispered.

Sarah nodded. She had been given a stay for her child to be born. As soon as they saw that her child had been born, that stay would be over.

And she would join her child.

CHAPTER 14

TWO WEEKS LATER

Reverend Parris himself stopped by Sarah's cell the morning of her execution. He nodded at her. "You and I will speak one last time." He nodded to the two guards he had brought with him.

Rebecca clutched Sarah's arm as Sarah stood. "I do not like this."

But even though she could sense Rebecca's fear for her, Sarah herself felt no fear, no anger, no sorrow, no pain. The truth was that since Mercy had been taken from her, she'd been nothing but blessedly numb. And all she felt was tired. Sarah patted Rebecca's hand. "Rest easy, friend. What more can they do to us now?"

And that was the truth. For even Rebecca had been sentenced to death. She would die later today alongside Sarah.

The guards led Sarah to the end of the hall and then into the church. They passed across the front and then into the hall that led to Samuel's office.

There was a closet halfway down.

"Stop here," Samuel ordered as he stepped forward. "You've

been asking about your daughter. I thought you might want to say good-bye." He pulled the door open.

The closet was dark inside. Sarah stepped forward as the smell hit her.

No.

Dorcas's dress reeked of urine and vomit. Her hair hung limp around her face, and she did not even look up as the light from the hallway hit her. Her dress hung on her, ripped and frayed.

Sarah moved as quickly as she could across the small space. "Dorcas, my love."

Her hands touched her daughter's face, but Dorcas did not respond. She stared straight ahead, drool leaking from the side of her mouth. "Oh, my beautiful girl, what have they done to you?"

"The fault for her condition lies with you."

Sarah whirled around. "How could you treat a child like this?"

He scoffed. "How could we? How could *you*? You refused to answer our questions. So we asked your daughter. She was more forthcoming." Samuel shrugged. "And this was the only place to put her. We couldn't put her in with the adults. We're not animals."

"Not animals!" Sarah lunged at him. "You bas—"

The guards quickly stepped in front of Sarah as he hastily backed away.

"Careful," he admonished, "or I will put you back in your cell. Now say thank you, witch, for me allowing this kindness of one last visit with your daughter."

Sarah glared at him.

"The words," he demanded.

"Thank you," she spit out through gritted teeth.

He smiled. "See? That was not so hard, was it?"

Sarah stared at the man in front of her. What had happened to him to make him so cruel? She turned back to Dorcas and pushed back her hair, her eyes filling with tears. She kissed her cheeks, whispering in her ear. "I love you, my beautiful girl. For all eternity. And we *will* see each other again."

Her daughter of light was now a shell. Her light had been completely snuffed out. That knowledge threatened to swallow Sarah whole, but at the same time she knew Dorcas never would have been spared. Ann would have made sure of that.

There was always a battle between good and evil forces in this world. But one day that final battle would be played out. And for the good to have any chance, the book needed to survive.

And I must remain silent, no matter the cost, she thought as her heart ached.

Right now she, Dorcas, Rebecca, and all the Followers were the soldiers on the front line. Right now the only weapon at their disposal was resistance.

She leaned her forehead into her daughter's, whispering softly so only she would hear. "You have done well, my child. But your fight is now over. You will be freed soon, and this will be just a horrible memory."

Dorcas did not stir. Sarah's heart clutched. Because she knew in that moment that while Dorcas's body would soon be freed, her mind would be forever locked in this cell.

"It's time," Samuel said, his tone hard.

Sarah reached up and ran her hand through her daughter's hair one more time, cupping her face, but her daughter still did not look at her.

Hide away, my dear. Hide away until the world is safe for you again. She kissed her cheek and then turned to Samuel.

He stood with a smug look on his face. "You could end all of this now. Tell me where the grimoire is and I will spare your life and your daughter's."

"Who told you I had a grimoire?"

"Ah, so you finally admit it."

"I admit nothing. But your accusation comes from somewhere. *Who* told you?"

His gaze shifted to the left for a fraction of a second before they returned to Sarah's eyes. "No one. It stands to reason if there is a coven, you would have book of spells." But his eyes told the truth. He was lying. *Stupid little man.* He was a pawn and didn't know it.

She turned and spared one last glance at her daughter before stepping into the hallway and heading back toward her cell. She didn't wait for her guards to instruct her.

"Stop." Samuel scrambled to catch up.

He had hoped to break her by showing her Dorcas, but it had only strengthened Sarah's resolve—and her anger. These men of God had tortured a child. They had tortured women with no power. And then claimed they were doing God's work. It was not God's work they did. It was the Fallen's. It was ignorance.

"You should repent while there is still time," Samuel said as he caught up with her.

Sarah stopped and looked pointedly at where her daughter was held and back at Samuel. "No, Reverend, you should be on your knees begging for forgiveness. Although I doubt even God could forgive what you've done here. It's not his work you do. The fires of Hell burn higher awaiting *your* arrival, not mine, and certainly not my daughter's."

And she swept past him, ready to meet her fate. She was done with this world.

CHAPTER 15

Sarah and Rebecca held their heads high as they walked from the cells to Gallows Hill. The other women sniffled behind them, crying and beseeching for forgiveness. Sarah couldn't condemn their fear. They had been taught they were unimportant, that they did not matter in this world beyond as an extension and example for their men in their family.

But the visit with her daughter coming on the heels of the death of her other daughter had snapped something inside of Sarah. She was truly done with this world. Done with anger, the hate, the bigotry. These small men running around thinking they were in charge when they were ruled by their own closed minds and a demon masquerading as a child.

Next to her, Rebecca gasped and stumbled. Sarah reached out a hand and caught her before she could fall. She looked up and saw Rebecca's husband, all of her children, and the oldest of her grandchildren.

Sarah leaned into her. "They love you, Rebecca. Let that love strengthen you. They are the legacy you leave behind, not this travesty of justice."

Rebecca nodded, even as tears rolled down her cheeks. Rebecca's case in particular *was* a travesty of justice. Rebecca had actually been found not guilty at first. But the girls had a fit in the courtroom and somehow the not guilty had been changed to a guilty verdict. And now here she walked with the other three who'd been found guilty: Sarah Wildes, Susannah Martin, and Elizabeth Howe.

Sarah stepped toward Rebecca to embrace her one last time, but a guard grabbed her by the arm, leading her to where the nooses had been fashioned. They stood blowing in the wind and Sarah was momentarily blinded by the vision of herself and the other women swinging just as briskly.

The judge and magistrates climbed onto the back of a wagon so they could see clearly. And even though their faces looked serious, she could imagine the joy in their eyes. They held the power of life and death in their hands. And they had wielded that power with a callous disregard for the truth.

One of the other women screamed, which set off the rest of the women, who all began to wail in earnest. Three women fell to their knees, their hands clasped, tears pouring down their cheeks. More than one prayed, begging God to forgive their accusers.

Sarah snorted, feeling no such charity for the men who'd placed them here. They'd be paying eternally for that particular action. Reverend Nicholas Noyes walked over to her, looking down his long spotted beak nose at her; the blood capsule had burst over the skin years ago.

"You should pray for forgiveness," he said. "God will not let you enter the kingdom of Heaven without it."

Sarah looked away from him.

"You will burn in Hell for all eternity for your actions. You should beg God to show compassion."

Sarah met his gaze unflinching, even as a vision of the man's death wafted through her mind. "Compassion for me? Or those who falsely accuse me? It seems my accusers should be the ones on their hands and knees begging for forgiveness, not I."

The reverend's mouth became a tight line. "Even now, your arrogance is your undoing. You are a witch and—"

Sarah snorted. "I am no more a witch than you are a wizard, and if you take away my life, God will give you blood to drink."

The reverend stumbled back, his hand to his throat. "You curse me, even now?"

She wanted to grab the man and slap some sense into him. "You are a fool and a sham. You do not do God's work here today. You do the Devil's. And you will pay the price for that one day, much more than I will."

"God have mercy on your soul."

"Save your pretty words for your own soul. You should pray, no, beg, that God has mercy on *yours*."

"Reverend, we are ready," Thomas Putnam said, his voice hard, but his eyes were harder as they glared at Sarah.

Weak, she thought. *You are weak. And your daughter is a monster.*

At the thought of Ann, her thoughts immediately turned to her youngest child, who had never had the chance to take a breath. Perhaps it was best that way. This world was too cruel right now for an innocent soul. Her last image of Dorcas flew into her mind and her heart broke, just as her daughter's mind had broken. They had terrified and tortured a child in the name of God and rightness. And they saw no hypocrisy in their actions.

Putnam grabbed her arm and started to pull her toward the gallows, where five ropes hung. She shrugged him off. "Do not *touch* me."

Thomas glared but let her walk unmolested. The other women were gathered and led to the hill. Each of them sobbed openly and loudly, needing to be practically carried to the hill. Even Rebecca shook, her strength fading at the sight of her family's devastated faces.

A crowd had gathered, split evenly between devastated family members and angry onlookers. After glancing at the Nurse family,

Sarah's gaze scanned the crowd although she knew no one was here for—

Her gaze flew back at the sight of a well-known and most loved face. Meg stood there, her eyes bright with tears, holding on to her grandfather.

Oh, child, you should not be here. Meg was not adept at hiding her emotions. Someone would question why she grieved for women she did not know. She stared into Meg's eyes. *Stay strong, child.*

As if hearing her, Meg lifted her chin and gave her a small nod. Sarah pulled her gaze away and faced the noose waiting for her. Images of her children flew through her mind. *Know that I loved you and I love you still,* she said to each of them in turn as the rope was slipped over her neck.

Then Sarah felt the shove and her feet swung out into open space. The rope tightened and her breath cut off, her lungs struggling to find air that would not come. The last image she had was of Dorcas, broken in her cell.

Forgive me, child. Forgive me.

CHAPTER 16

Meg paced her small attic room. *They're gone. They're all gone.* She pictured Sarah Goode's face; the commitment on it even as the noose was slipped over her neck.

I am not strong enough, Sarah.

All of the Followers had been arrested now, along with dozens of other. Six had been hung. Sarah Goode's baby and Susan Osbourne had died in prison.

There was no one left, save her.

I need to move the book. But she didn't know where to put it.

The bodies of her sisters had been buried where they'd fallen at Gallows Hill. Surely she could not bury the book there. It would be discovered. Fear choked her and she felt as if the walls were closing in. *What do I do?* She yanked on her hair, her breaths coming out in pants. How was this possible? All of them gone.

All except me.

Their loss crashed down on her, but so too did the responsibility. *I have to protect the book.* She knew where the book was hidden, but she could think of nowhere to put it where future generations could find it.

If I fail, the world will lose her, too, she thought with despair. She knew that could not happen. Right now, the world felt cruel, unkind. But these dark times would end. Good would shine through if enough good people stood up. Tears flowed down her cheeks. *But how will I help fight it back?*

The front door slammed and footsteps moved toward the stairs. From the dragging gait, she knew it was her grandfather, but his steps were quicker, more urgent. *Oh no.* Wiping her tears, she opened her door and hurried down her steep staircase. She stepped onto the second floor landing just as he reached it. He put one hand to his chest, the other grabbing onto the bannister. His knuckles, swollen from the arthritis that plagued him, stood out white against his skin.

"Child," he panted out.

Hurrying forward, she took his arm and led him into his room and the chair there. "Grandfather, are you all right? Let me get you some water."

She turned to fill him a glass of water from the pitcher on the dresser, but he grabbed her arm stopping her with surprising speed. "There is no time for that." He took a deep breath and she waited while he composed himself.

"I am barely ahead of them. The magistrate—they are coming. You have been accused."

Meg stumbled back. "What?"

"Reverend Samuel is on his way with Thomas Putnam and others."

Meg looked around wildly. *It's too late. How can—*

Her grandfather squeezed her arm. "You must give them a name."

"No, Grandfather, I can't do that. Witches do not exist. I'd be accusing an innocent woman."

"Then give them a man. There are plenty who are *not* innocent."

Meg stared at him as if seeing him for the first time. "Why would you say that?"

He looked out the window before turning back to her. "You are your mother's child. And she was her mother's. Your grandmother told me about the Followers a long time ago. I never interfered. The more your grandmother told me, the more I agreed with the teachings."

"You never said anything."

"No. I thought it was safer, for all of you."

"They're all gone, Grandfather, and I have to—" She slammed her mouth shut. It had been ingrained into her from an early age to never speak of the duty of the Followers.

He patted her hand. "I know there are things you cannot tell me. But I also know how important whatever you are guarding is. You are the last one. The duty falls to you."

Meg's voice broke. "I cannot do this."

"You can. You have the strength of your mother and grandmother in you. And some of mine as well. You *can* do this." He paused gripping her hand. "And I want you to give them my name."

She snatched her hand back. "No!"

"I have lived a full life. My bones ache. It is difficult to walk even a flight of stairs. And I would like to see your grandmother and mother again. My time is at an end, and if my death can be used for a greater good, than I cannot think of a better death."

Tears rolled down Meg's face. "I would be responsible for your death."

"No, child. That burden is on Reverend Samuel and the rest who engage in this farce. You, you would be responsible for setting me free from my pain. *That* will be a gift."

Movement outside the window pulled Meg's attention. Samuel was making his way down the small lane to their house. "They are coming."

Her grandfather stood. "You will give them my name and complete your duty. If you do not, I will confess to being a wizard and I will die anyway. You can give my death meaning, or you can make it as senseless as everyone else's. But you cannot prevent it."

He walked out of the room, his walk much slower as he started down the stairs.

Samuel pushed open the gate outside.

I cannot change any of this, Meg thought wildly. And then she pictured her grandfather, his resolve and the resolve of her sisters. She straightened her shoulders even as her heart shredded into millions of pieces. *I am the descendant of a long line of strong women. I will not fail them.*

She quickly ran down the stairs and stood next to her grandfather, who stood waiting at the front door. She placed her hand in his and then leaned up and kissed his cheek. He looked down at her in surprise and then smiled.

A loud rap sounded at the door. He squeezed her hand, and she felt the tremor in his. But she heard the message he was sending. They were not words said very often in their community. She squeezed his hand back in answer.

I love you, too, Grandfather.

CHAPTER 17

THREE WEEKS LATER

The courtroom was packed and the gallery silenced for a moment as Meg was led in before the noise ratcheted back up. Putnam pushed Meg forward toward the seat next to the dais.

Meg's trial had finally arrived. She had been locked up for over three weeks now. She thought they had forgotten about her, which would have been understandable as they had arrested so many people in that time. Cells were packed. In Meg's cell, the women took turns sleeping. There was simply not enough room for all of them to lie down at the same time.

Food had been another problem. Not all the women in her cell could afford to pay for food. Most shared what little they had but more than one fight had broken out when one person accused another of taking more than their fair share.

They have reduced us to animals.

Now she sat in front of the 'good' townsfolk of Salem. The people who had known her her whole life. She had played with their children, sat next to them at church, shared a meal with them. And now they stared back at her with angry contempt.

The magistrate didn't even look at her as she took her seat, although he did nod at Putnam before he banged his gavel. "The Special Court of Oyer and Terminer is now in session. All who wish to bear witness may be heard."

The court gallery quieted, and Meg scanned it before latching on to her grandfather's face. He sat at the end of the second row. He gave her a nod.

Meg was so nervous she didn't dare nod back, lest it be taken as some sort of confession. Last night had easily been the worst night since she'd been locked up. Dorcas had joined their cell.

Almost everyone had been shocked into silence at the sight of her. Her dress was tattered beyond repair. Her hair hung matted on her head. And her bones were displayed painfully through her skin. They had all thought she would be released after Sarah's death. But apparently her father had not come across with enough money and she was to be held a few days longer.

The girl didn't speak. She didn't move. The women in the cell with her each took turns trying to feed her and get her to drink. Still, she had taken very little. To see someone so small treated so cruelly; it would draw compassion from the darkest of hearts.

But not from these men—these men who said they were looking for monsters. They *were* the monsters. Dorcas's mind was already broken. Even if she left the prison one day, she would never be normal, not after this.

But it wasn't just Dorcas condition that had kept her awake. She had tried and tried to figure out a way to protect the book and her grandfather. She should have told him where it was, let him move it. But even if she had, with his health, he would not be up to the task. She had struggled trying to find some way to spare him and still stay true to their duty.

For a dark moment, she had even considered turning her back on her duty. But in her heart, in her soul she knew the book would one day change the course of the world, and she could not be the one who helped evil win.

"Sister Jacobs," Magistrate Hathorne said, his voice deep and cold, "you have been accused of being a witch—a serious charge. But perhaps," he said softly, his tone shifting, "you are not a witch but the victim of one. You are young, impressionable. A witch could easily hold sway on such an innocent young woman. Tell us the name of the witch who has plagued you and I will see you freed."

The audience murmured, nodding their heads. Meg could not tell if they agreed with Hathorne or not. But she also knew that this was the moment she had been dreading. Others had provided names to secure their own release—it was why the jail was so crowded. She had accepted that for her to fulfill her mission, she must provide a name.

But now that the moment was here, Meg could not seem to get her mouth to work. She was going to accuse an innocent man in court. She could not do that. She shook her head.

"I order you to tell us the name." He leaned forward, his voice venomous. "Or declare yourself a witch and face the consequences."

Meg's chest ached, her eyes stung, and she stared at the gallery, full of people who'd, almost as one, leaned forward to hear her reply. No one jumped to her defense. She'd spent her whole life here and all the good people of Salem had turned their backs on her.

Then her eyes locked on her grandfather's. He gripped the back of the bench in front of him, staring intensely at her. And then he started to stand.

"George Burroughs!" she yelled. Her grandfather froze and then slowly lowered himself back to the bench.

The magistrate turned back to her, surprise on his face. "The *Reverend* George Burroughs?"

Meg nodded slowly. "Yes," she whispered. Last night she realized if she had to give them a name, it should be someone who was beyond their reach. The reverend had moved to Wells,

Maine. It seemed unlikely they would go all that way to retrieve him.

The magistrate walked slowly across the front of the room, his hand on his chin as he spoke. "The Reverend Burroughs. He was here for three years before he left." He looked to Samuel, who stood.

"I have heard his name before mumbled by others," Samuel said. "I believe him to be the ringleader of the witches."

A rumble rolled through the crowd in attendance as they digested this new piece of information. Meg felt sick. He was an innocent man—just as she was an innocent woman. But no one was interested in that truth.

The magistrate nodded sagely. "A ringleader, of course. For these witches, although filled with the Devil, are also women and therefore need a man to be in charge."

Nods from the audience followed his words, and Meg could swear she heard Sarah Goode laugh in her mind. *Men indeed.*

But although she hated what she had done, she knew it would allow her to leave prison. Others had done the same. And once she had left, she would recant. She would not let the lie stand. But first she must protect the legacy.

The magistrate made some notes on a paper. Meg closed her hands together. *Please let this be over. Please let that be enough.*

A shriek went up from the audience, and Meg's hand flew to her chest. Abigail Williams and Ann Putnam dropped to the floor, shrieking. A second later, Mercy Lewis and Mary Warren did as well. The people around them leaped to their feet, backing away while making the sign of the cross.

Samuel leaped to his feet as well, but he stormed to the gate that kept the audience back. "There is another!"

Meg's eyes went wide and her breathing all but stopped.

The magistrate walked quickly over to him. "Another?"

Samuel nodded, gesturing to the girls. "Someone else plagues them." As if on cue, the girls stopped their theatrics.

The magistrate turned back to Meg. "There is another," he said quietly.

The girls rose shakily to their feet, but the people of Salem didn't move closer. The girls collapsed on the benches, leaning against one another.

Meg swallowed heavily as her grandfather nodded at her. *No*, she begged him silently. *Don't make me do this.*

He nodded at her again as if he could read her mind, his face serious.

The magistrate walked slowly across the room toward her. "Sister Jacobs, it seems you have forgotten to mention someone."

Meg shook her head, tears pressing against the back of her eyes. "No."

"Really? Well, perhaps we should question you in more depth, in private."

Meg's heart began to race. She shook her head wildly. Dorcas had been 'privately' questioned. Meg's eyes flew to her grandfather, and she saw the determination on his face. He would not let her face this. He would either stand by her side or in her place.

You cannot prevent it.

He started to stand again, and her heart broke. She was going to lose him. She could not change that. But she could protect the legacy. Squeezing her hands shut, her nails broke the skin and blood seeped across her palm. She nodded slowly. "My—"

She stopped licking her lips, her heart pounding so hard she thought it would explode. She wished it would explode because then this burden would not be hers.

But it didn't. It continued to beat, the traitorous organ. So she straightened her shoulders, picturing her grandfather reuniting with his wife and daughter. But even with that comforting image in her mind, her voice was still a whisper.

"My grandfather."

CHAPTER 18

Meg had not been released right after her trial. She had been held for another three days. And for those three days she replayed the image of her grandfather being pulled from the court over and over in her mind.

At that moment, she had barely been able to contain the scream that wanted to burst from her chest, demanding they release him, letting them all know she had lied. But her grandfather's gaze had remained fixed on her, warning her without words not to speak. Tears had trailed down her cheeks as she watched him get pulled away.

"There, there, my dear," the magistrate had said. "Take solace that your grandfather no longer inhabits that vessel. And soon the vessel itself will be destroyed."

Meg had not known if he thought his words would offer her comfort or if he was being intentionally cruel.

This morning when she had stepped out of the courthouse, it had been quiet. She knew more trials had been conducted and were in fact going on right now. But she was numb to it all. If the trials worked as usual, her grandfather would be tried in two months' time. But she planned on getting him released long before that.

She would move the book and recant.

No matter what he said, she would not have his death be caused by her words. Even knowing she needed to move quickly to set things into motion, she walked slowly down the steps, grateful for the solitude, her mind spinning. She was not up to speaking with anyone at the moment. She was exhausted both physically and spiritually. And hunger was sapping what little strength she did have. She would go home, eat, rest, and then get to work.

"Hello, Meg."

Meg whirled around at the voice, her hand to her throat. Ann Putnam sat on the horse railing, one leg swinging as she watched Meg.

"Ann, you scared me. I did not see you there."

Ann hopped off the railing. "Perhaps I did not want you to see me. Perhaps I was invisible."

Meg backed away as the girl approached. She had never liked Ann. The girl had always been too arrogant, and her parents had indulged her, much more than Puritans normally would. But now there was something else about the girl—something colder, darker.

"Where are you going?" Ann asked.

"H—home."

Ann nodded her head before tilting it to the side. "It will be awfully quiet there now, yes?"

Meg didn't know what to say so she simply turned away from the strange girl and started walking quickly toward her house. A rock slammed into her shoulder, causing her to stumble.

Meg whirled around. "Did you just throw a rock at me?"

Ann tossed a rock from side to side in her hand. "Did I? The Devil must have made me do it."

"Do you *want* something, Ann?"

Ann moved toward her quickly, standing too close to Meg. "I want to know why you accused your grandfather. I didn't see his spirit attack anyone. Neither did the other girls."

Meg backed away. "Mer—Mercy said she did."

Ann nodded. "True, but that's only because I told her to."

"Why would you do that?"

"Because you obviously wanted him in jail and yourself out. And I have to wonder why. What are hiding, Meg?" Meg's blood ran cold as Ann leaned in and whispered, "Or have you not hidden it yet?"

Meg stared at her, her heart racing. "Who are you?"

Ann smiled. "You know, Sarah Goode asked me exactly the same question when I first spoke with her. I am an old, old friend of the Followers."

"Where is Ann?"

Ann laughed. "Very good. Not even Sarah seemed to realize that Ann is no longer here. Well, that is not entirely true. She is here, just not able to speak. I can feel her, her terror. She does not like sharing this space with me. But soon enough, she will not have to. It will just be me."

"And what will happen to Ann?"

"She will die."

"How is this possible?"

"Tituba. She opened a door in Ann's mind. Ann is a descendant of an ancient race. She has no idea. None of the Putnams do. But once the door opened, I zipped in, knowing my chance was here. And that my liege would be so happy for the knowledge I could tell him the next time we meet."

"I—I thought you did not remember your former lives."

Ann shrugged. "Normally we do not. But I was never supposed to be in this body. So I believe there is a chance I will remember."

"A chance? You are doing all this for a chance?"

Ann shrugged. "What can I say? I am an optimist."

Meg started to back away from the demon in front of her. "I will not tell you."

"Oh yes, you will."

"No, you and your master can go back to Hell."

"Oh I do not think that's our fate. We are fated to live here, to rule here, while you humans all scurry to do our bidding."

Meg trembled, her knees going weak. "What is your name?"

"Another question Sarah asked me, but I never told her—there was no point." She eyed Meg, "But you, I think you scare more easily."

Meg swallowed hard, even knowing the action answered Ann's question. And at the same time knowing it was probably best if she did not know which of the Fallen stood before her.

Ann leaned forward. "I am Azazyel."

Meg gasped, stumbling, her hand to her chest. Azazyel, Samyaza's right-hand man, his most loyal and deadly soldier.

"Ann!"

Meg's gaze jolted to her right, where Thomas and Ann Putnam stood, neither looking happy. Thomas strode up. "Do not speak to my daughter," he hissed.

Meg backed away, fearful of the anger in his voice.

"Did she hurt you?" Ann Sr. asked.

Ann's whole face changed. Her eyes became fearful, her voice timid. "No, Mother. But she is not right."

With another glare at Meg, Thomas took Ann by the arm and led her down the road. Ann Sr. stood protectively on her other side. Ann looked over her shoulder and winked back at Meg. And Meg heard the words Ann mouthed as if she had said them aloud.

See you soon.

CHAPTER 19

Meg wasn't sure how she made it home. Between the fear coursing through her from her run-in with Ann and the fear of what was happening to her grandfather, she didn't know how she was still standing.

There was something inside of Ann Putnam. But it was not the Devil. It was a Fallen angel, one of the worst—Azazyel. He was said to have taught humanity war craft. And to have even shared the secrets of witchcraft and led them into wickedness.

He had somehow taken advantage of Ann. What had Tituba done? How had she opened a door? And Ann, poor Ann, somehow still alive inside with that… thing.

She had heard of people being possessed, but she knew it was not a simple undertaking. But what could Meg do about it? No one would believe her. Ann/Azazyel had everyone believing she could see the true witches. Meg would only get thrown back in prison if she said anything.

In shock, she looked up and saw she had arrived at her home. She pushed open the gate, suddenly exhausted. Her legs seemed to get heavier and heavier as she approached the door. She all but fell into it and pushed. It opened and she stumbled in.

She leaned heavily on the door after she shut it. *I need to get the book.* She knew that was true. But she had not slept in days. She was in no condition for the task ahead of her. And she'd need to wait until long after dark to make sure she wasn't seen.

She looked at the stairs, dreaming of her bed, but she was too tired to climb them. And besides, she would have to pass her grandfather's room and she did not think she could face that right now. Instead she walked over to the rocking chair, the one her great grandfather had crafted. Grabbing a quilt from the basket by the cold fireplace, she sat down, pulling the quilt over her. It would get cold tonight, and she should make a fire, but she did not have the energy now. She pictured her grandfather and imagined him standing on a chair at Gallows Hill.

Pulling the quilt to her chin, she squeezed her eyes tight, trying to shut away the image. Tears pressed against the back of her lids.

Oh, please no, she begged, knowing once she started crying she would be unable to stop the sobs. But fate proved merciful, because while she did begin to cry, she also slept. She slept through the long afternoon and through the dark night—a deep and dreamless sleep.

CHAPTER 20

Meg jerked awake, her heart pounding as she looked around. *Home, I am home,* she thought as she stared at the light coming in through the windows, reality slowly returning. Her back ached from the uncomfortable sleeping position but even so, she wanted to sleep longer. But her rumbling stomach wouldn't let her. Stumbling to the kitchen, she made herself two biscuits with the last of the flour. She washed it down with some water and then went back to the rocking chair and let sleep reclaim her.

She didn't awake again until it was dark. She stared around the room trying to see what had awakened her. A chill crawled over her skin and she pulled the quilt tighter around her. *It's nothing. Go back to sleep,* she told herself.

The unease didn't lessen. She went and checked the locks and stared out each window. She knew it was just her imagination, but she still had trouble settling down.

By the time dawn broke, she had been awake for hours. She took some of her grandfather's coins to buy bread and some vegetables for soup. She left early, hoping she would be able to get her business done before anyone was up. She also stopped at the post office and dropped off a letter for her cousin in Boston. She should know what had happened to them here. The small farm would be hers once Meg was gone.

She had just stepped out of the post office when an arm slipped through hers. "There you are."

Meg looked down at Ann in horror and tried to pull her arm away from her, but she wouldn't let her.

Ann shook her head. "Tsk, tsk. Is that any way to treat a friend? Especially one who has been so concerned for you? Why, I must have stood by the old willow tree behind your house for hours these last two nights. You know, to make sure if you went for a late night walk you did not hurt yourself."

Meg gasped. She had felt eyes on her but thought she was being paranoid. She tried again to pull her arm away, but Ann held her too tight. "So have you heard the big news?"

"Wh—what news?"

"Why, George Burroughs has been brought back from Maine."

Meg stopped dead. "What?"

"I can see you are relieved. After all, you *were* the one who accused him. Thank goodness he has been brought to justice and is not free to defile other young ladies." Ann wiggled her eyebrows at Meg.

"He is here? But how?"

"Well, the magistrate sent a special contingent. After all, he *is* the ringleader."

"Ringleader?"

"A funny thing happened while you were convalescing. The other girls and I realized it was Burroughs behind all of it after all. His specter visited each of us."

"Wh—when will he be tried?"

"Oh, he's already been tried and found guilty—your grandfather as well. With so many people in prison, I suppose they realized they really need to hurry these trials along. Oh look, that is them there." Ann pointed down the street. A crowd waited around the prison. She had been so focused on Ann, Meg hadn't heard them. An angry roar went up as the door opened and her grandfather stepped out, two men gripping him on either side. Meg's knees gave out and she sank to the ground.

Ann knelt next to her. "Oh no. Are you all right?"

Meg tried to push her away. "Please just leave me alone."

"Not until you give me what I want. Tell me where the book is and I will go right now and tell them all your grandfather, the reverend, all of them, are innocent."

Meg stared into the face of the girl. She was beautiful, and yet her eyes were dead. The book was more than a chronicling of the Great Mother. It was a tool to fight the Fallen. And if the Fallen got their hands on it, that fight would be lost.

And so would humanity.

Her grandfather was lost in the crowd as three other men were pushed out with him, and then Reverend Burroughs. The crowd pushed them along the street, heading to Gallows Hill. There was nothing that would stop them now.

Meg pushed herself to her feet, unsure what to do. She wanted to stand by her grandfather. To offer him the comfort he had provided her. But he would not want that because he knew she would not be able to stand quietly as he took his last breaths. And then she would endanger herself.

"Where is the book?"

Meg looked down at the demon standing next to her. "I will never tell you. I will die first."

Ann watched her quietly for a moment, sending a new chill through Meg. "Yes, I think you will," she said quietly before walking away.

CHAPTER 21

The murmurs of the crowd that lined the street was muted, just a faint buzz of noise as Cotton walked toward Gallows Hill. Reverend Samuel Parrish was next to him, and ahead of them were the men to be hung today including the Reverend George Burroughs. To date, six witches had been put to death. For the first time since the trials began, however, it was men who would be hung.

Cotton had been unable to attend the other executions, but he had wanted to see one live and in person. *This one holds extra appeal,* he thought as he glared at Reverend Burroughs's back. He had never liked the man. His teachings were unorthodox, his manner too casual. Now he knew why. The Devil was in the man. Not only that, but he was the leader of the witches. The man should be burnt instead of hung.

A crowd followed behind them and another already waited at the Hill. As soon as they caught sight of Burroughs, the cries began. "Mercy! Have mercy!"

Cotton stared at them in shock. Did they not know who they had in their midst? The cries continued, an indecipherable yell, but every once in while a cry would rise up above the din.

"Spare him! He is a man of God."

Cotton strode forward. They had gone too far. He held up his hands. "People, good people of Salem. Listen to me! Listen!"

The crowd quieted to a murmur.

Cotton glanced across the crowd. "The Devil is a tricky beast. He will hide behind the face of those you trust most. He will use the vestiges of even a reverend to lull you into his clutches. Do you wish for your children to be put into the Devil's care?"

He glared at Burroughs, who now stood on a chair, the noose around his neck, the executioner behind him. "Do not be fooled by this man's past. He is a reverend no longer. The name of God is poison in his mouth. He cannot even stand to—"

Burroughs glared right back at Cotton, not letting him look away. "Our Father, who art in heaven, hallowed be thy name . . . "

A gasp went up across the crowd as Burroughs continued to say the Lord's prayer. Even Cotton was shaken. It should not be possible. The Lord's words should burn on his tongue.

"Blasphemous," Samuel cursed and Cotton could feel his anger.

Burroughs finished the prayer calmly. "I am no demon. The Devil does not dwell within me."

Burroughs's words rallied the crowd and they began to mutter. The executioner standing behind Burroughs glanced at Samuel, who nodded. He pushed Burroughs off the chair and the crowd gasped in horror.

"We will lose them," Samuel hissed in Cotton's ear. "Do something."

Cotton batted him away. He did not care for the reverend. The man was too single minded in his focus, almost a fanatic. But he *was* right about the crowd. Cotton stepped forward again and raised his voice to be heard clearly. "Good people of Salem. This is but a trick. Remember the Devil has often been transformed into an Angel of Light. Burroughs was no longer a man of God but a tool of Satan. What we do here today is God's work."

The crowd quieted and Cotton continued to speak, reminding

the crowd of the innocent victims and the true test of courage they now faced. The crowd finally calmed and the other four executions went off without any issues. Shortly thereafter, the crowds dispersed until only Cotton remained. He stared up at George Burroughs. He did not doubt his own words. The Devil could take the shape of a good man. But the words, how had Burroughs said the words?

A wind blew, cutting through his clothes and sending a chill through him. He turned and headed for town, his head down.

It was God's work we did. God's *work.*

But even in his mind he heard the doubt underlying the words.

CHAPTER 22

Meg made her way home, the food in her basket no longer calling to her, her appetite gone. *Grandfather.* Tears streamed down her face, making it difficult to walk. In town, she could hear the crowd but she could not bring herself to watch, even though she had turned toward Gallows Hill and begun to walk more than once. But she had known if she had seen her grandfather, she would have been unable to stay silent. And his sacrifice would have been for nothing.

The truth of that did not however ease the guilt and pain that curled through her with every step she took away from him. When she had seen her home on the distance, she'd begun to shake. By the time she had reached the door, she was trembling so hard she could barely get the door open. She'd just managed to stumble in before the sobs overtook her and she crashed to the floor. *I can't do this.*

She sat for hours on the floor as she shook and sobbed, until finally she just lay curled up, staring into space. She was the weakest of the Followers. She knew that. They all had known that. Sarah could have done this. Rebecca, Mary—any of them would have already hidden the book. They would have spat in Azazyel's face. But she, Meg, was too terrified to move. Terrified of Azazyel, terrified that she would fail and be caught. Terrified that she simply wasn't enough.

Ann was watching the house. How was Meg supposed to get to the book without her knowing? She couldn't lead her to it.

Oh, sisters, I don't want to fail you.

Meg didn't fear dying. At this point, it would be a blessing. She, the least worthy, had survived while the others had perished. And now she would fail them all. Meg curled up on the floor, indecision and impotence paralyzing her.

I can't do this. I can't—

"Of course you can."

Meg's head shot up as Sarah took a seat at the table. "Sarah?"

Sarah waved her over. "Come on. We don't have a lot of time."

Meg scrambled to her feet and flung herself at Sarah. "You're alive. You escaped."

Sarah shook her head. "No. child. I did not."

Meg pulled back. "But how?"

"That is not the question you really want to ask, is it?"

Meg shook her head. "There is a Fallen here. He has possessed Ann Putnam. I do not know how to get around him. He will stop me."

"No, he will not. You are stronger than he is."

"No, I am scared and weak."

"You cannot be brave without being scared. And you are not weak. You do not see yourself as I do. As we all do. You are a descendant of warriors. We all see that strength."

Tears blurred Meg's vision. "I am not strong. I am going to fail you."

"You could never fail us, no matter the outcome. You have been taught by some of the greatest women. You know what to do. You just need to think it through. You have the answers. Your fear is just blocking them from your view."

"How do I look beyond it?

"First, you look inside and see who you are, not who the world tells you you are. But who you truly know yourself to be. That is who will succeed. For she is magnificent." Sarah's eyes shone brightly.

"I miss you. I miss all of you."

"We are always with you. Your sisters have never left you. They stand beside you wherever you go. We are one."

"We are one," Meg repeated as a rumble of thunder rolled across the sky.

Meg's head jerked up from her spot by the door.

We are one. The words floated through her mind as she glanced over at the empty chair by the table. Sadness fell over her. *It was just a dream.* But she realized that wasn't true, either. It wasn't just a dream. It was a visit.

Meg stood up, resolve filling her. One way or another, she was going to end this tonight. She picked up her basket and moved to the table, pulling out the food she had picked up earlier.

First, I need a good meal to strengthen me. And then I need a plan.

CHAPTER 23

Sarah's visit *had* renewed Meg. But as darkness began to fall, so too did her resolve, and that was when Benjamin Nurse and his son brought her grandfather home. They'd taken him to the family cemetery and begun digging. Good manners dictated that Meg go outside and offer them a drink, but she could not bring herself to face them. She could not bear to see the pity, anger, or accusation in their eyes.

But once they had left, she stepped quietly outside. And even though it was not cold, she felt a chill over her skin. She walked slowly to the family plot and pushed open the gate. They had buried him next to her grandmother. *He would like that*, she thought with a small smile. But the image of her grandfather when she'd last seen him tore through her. He was gone. He had been her strength. She stumbled toward the newly dug grave. She collapsed on top of it, her legs no longer able to support her.

I did this to you. Then the memories of the horror since all this began fell over her and she sobbed and sobbed, not sure if she would ever be able to stop. They were all dead. Her grandfather was dead by her hand, or close enough. Even poor Reverend Burroughs.

The dark finally sent her back inside, but Meg did not turn on any lights. She sat in the dark and thought of her sisters, her mother, her grandmother. She let the lessons they had taught her wash over her and let herself grieve for them. She even fell asleep for a little while, curled up next to the cold fireplace. And when she had awoken, the remnants of a dream stayed with her. It was from a lesson Rebecca had taught her from the book. She sat there in the dark thinking in through. *Is it possible?* She was not sure if it would work but she would try. She could think of no other way to stop this blight.

She reached up into the fireplace and felt for the loose brick. Pulling it free, she let the brick drop before reaching in and pulling out the cloth. Pulling back the layers, she felt the design of the pendant lying there—two intertwined triangles. She slipped the necklace over her neck and grabbed her grandfather's satchel from the cupboard.

Before she could allow the doubts to creep in, she slipped from the house. She did not know if Ann was nearby watching her. She hoped she was. The sooner she could confront her the sooner this would all end, one way or the other.

Meg hurried down the road and then carefully cut across the field that bordered the Nurse plantation. Her heart clutched at the thought of Rebecca, but she shoved it aside. *I will grieve later*, she promised herself.

She walked beyond the border of Rebecca's land and into the wild forest that bordered it. Her steps slowed as the way became more difficult. She stepped over a downed tree and her dress ripped on an extended branch. She yanked it from the snare and heard it rip, but she pushed on, not even bothering to examine the damage.

Ahead, the cave loomed, and Meg went still. She pulled the candle and flint from her satchel. Bringing up a flame quickly, she lit the candle. A soft glow embraced the surrounding area but also darkened the shadows beyond the light's reach.

She swallowed. *I will not be afraid*. She repeated the words over and over as she made her way to the cave. She only let herself pause for a moment at its entrance before stepping quickly inside. The flame cast dancing shadows along the long, narrow cave's walls. She hurried as quickly as she dared with the dim light. Three hundred feet in she stopped at a protuberance that caused one to crouch. She ducked under and then placed the candle on the ground. Reaching up, she strained to reach the small empty space hidden behind the rock face.

Come on.

Stretching as far as she could, her shoulder beginning to ache with the effort, her fingers touched canvas bag. She reached in and pulled it out. Then she stretched up again and pulled out a long, thin piece of wire. Grasping her finds to her chest, she sat on the ground, brushing at the dirt until three small holes were revealed.

Meg emptied the contents of the bag into her hand. She straightened the rope, and three L-shaped pieces of metal glinted back at her. Meg slid each piece of metal into the longer piece and locked them in place.

She lined the long metal piece over the holes and inserted the smaller leg into the three holes. She pushed down and right until the lock clicked in place. Rotating the metal rod to the left, she felt the covering give way. Shifting to a crouch, she pulled the circular covering off and placed it to the side.

With a trembling breath, she peered into the small recess that had been hidden. A burlap sack lay there and she let out a breath. She pulled it out with trembling hands.

She had never been the one to remove the book, although she had watched the others with awe when they had done so. She missed them so much in that moment and felt so alone. *I will see them soon*. Reaching inside the sack, she felt the edges of the box. Pulling it out, the candlelight reflected off the ivory box, causing sparkles of light to shoot across the space.

Despite the horror of the last few days and months, she smiled. It looked magical. And she remembered when she'd first seen it. She had been sure she had never seen anything more beautiful. She ran a hand over the box, tracing some of the scenes from the Great Mother's many lives.

Then she opened the box, and inside lay the *Tome of the Great Mother*. Meg just stared for a moment at the unassuming brown leather cover before reaching in with a trembling hand and pulling it out. Flipping it open, the plain cover gave way to intricately designed pages. Drawings, first in color then black and white, adorned each page. The words on the first few pages she could not read. Sarah had planned on teaching her in the next few years.

Meg took a breath at the stab of fresh grief that rolled through her. *Not the time*, she reminded herself as she continued to flip, looking for a specific page.

Her eyes finally landed on it. Susan had shown her this page two years ago, when Meg had been officially inducted into the Followers. All inductees were shown the book and taught its lessons, as well as being shown its hiding place. This page had not held Meg's interest. She had been more intrigued by the tales of the Great Mother's various incarnations. But now she greedily read through it, squinting and shifting to make out the words in the dim light.

She read the page five times, committing it to memory before she closed the book. Carefully placing the book back in its box, she placed it in the sack it had been hidden in and then placed that in her satchel. Looping the satchel over her head, she stood, stumbling a little under the weight of the it.

Picking up the candle, she made her way to the entrance, her mind reciting everything from the page. She paused in her ruminations as she stepped from the cave and listened, but she heard no sounds.

No sounds at all.

A tickle of fear breathed across her neck. And then Ann stepped into the light of the candle.

"There you are."

CHAPTER 24

Even though she had been expecting her, the sight of Ann still terrified Meg. She knew who she was now, what she was. She pictured Tituba and the other girl accusers.

Oh, girls, if only you hadn't played with things beyond your comprehension.

But she supposed she couldn't blame them. Women in Salem led such rigid lives, with little chance for adventure, curiosity, or even happiness. She could see why the dark arts would appeal to them. Something dangerous, something forbidden.

But the cost of that rebellion had been cast in blood. *And now, all my sisters are gone,* Meg thought, staring at the beast in a familiar face. *And I will be joining them soon enough.*

Ann hopped further into the circle of light and twirled around. "I had forgotten how enjoyable these bodies are. You feel everything—the wind on your skin, the scents of fresh bread, and the emotions. It's amazing."

"You have never felt emotions before?"

"I have. But before we fell, there were none save envy. Envy of you *apes* and your freedoms. But I can appreciate those emotions now. They heighten everything. Why, these last few months have brought me such joy; it has been hard to contain." She straightened out her skirt. "Of course, I can laugh out loud and everyone will think the Devil made me do it. It *is* freeing."

"What do you want, Azazyel?"

"Why, that little book you have hidden in the satchel, of course. It is practically singing to me."

Meg shook her head. "I will not give it to you."

Ann smiled. "Of course you will. You traded your own grandfather for your freedom. You are not the type to sacrifice yourself. Now hand it over before I feel the need to point a finger at you."

Meg clutched the satchel to her. "They will not believe you. I have been freed."

"So was Rebecca. And then they changed their minds. The only reason you were let go was so you would retrieve the book for me."

"Why do you want it so much? What is so important about it for you?"

"That is not your concern."

Meg tilted her head, studying the beast in front of her. "You're scared of it. Something in this book terrifies you."

Ann's eyes became narrow slits. "I am done with this conversation. Hand over the book or pay the consequences."

Meg trembled at the venom in her tone. "All right. But you promise, I will go free?"

Ann smiled. "Of course. You help me and I shall help you."

Meg gripped the satchel, the legacy she and her sisters had sacrificed for eons to protect. And all of that preparation had come to this one moment. It had come down to Meg.

The responsibility of this moment and the fear was almost overwhelming.

I am not worthy of making this choice, she thought desperately.

Ann took a small step forward as if approaching a wounded animal. "Come now, Meg. We can end all of this right now. You do not want this burden. You have never wanted it. And why should you? In the name of a woman long dead, whom you will never meet? Who does not care about you? No. Live your life, Meg. Live it free of this burden. Embrace what life has to offer."

The words were tempting. Letting it all go. Unlike the other sisters, she had always been terrified by the responsibility laid upon them.

"Give it here, Meg. You are the last. They have gotten all the rest. You are alone, just one scared, terrified girl. Hand that over and your fears are over. You can live in peace."

"You—you promise?"

Ann inched closer. "Of course, child. You are not important. You have never been important, none of you have. It is the book that I want. Give it to me and all this is finished with."

Meg nodded, her voice trembling. "Here. I never wanted this responsibility." She stepped forward and extended the satchel forward. "Take it."

Ann's eyes fixated on the satchel. She smiled, moving forward quickly. She snatched the bag and pulled it to her.

But Meg gripped her arm, wrapping the necklace around both of their wrists, trapping them together.

"What are you doing?"

"Sending you back." And then she began to repeat the words that she had memorized from the book. "Spirit of darkness, inhabit this soul no longer. Find this vessel blocked from your evil. Pain and darkness will be all you will feel in this place."

Ann screamed as the pendant began to glow. Meg grimaced as the heat began to burn her arm, but she didn't let go. And she could swear she felt the hands of her sisters on her shoulder, giving her their strength.

"Be gone from this place. Leave this soul alone. In the name of the Great Mother, I banish you now and forever."

Meg repeated the words over and over. Ann screamed and yanked on her arm. "Let me go! Release me!"

The amulet heated up so much it glowed bright orange. But

Meg barely felt it. "Be gone from this place. Leave this soul alone. In the name of the Great Mother, I banish you now and forever."

A blinding light burst from the amulet and Meg cried out as she was thrown back. Ann screamed as well, landing across from Meg.

The air rushed from Meg's lungs and she gasped but no air came. She climbed to her knees and struggled to breathe. And then, blessedly, the air returned. She turned her head. Ann lay on the ground only a few feet away. Fire seemed to burn under her skin along her veins, making her glow bright.

Ann turned her head to glare at Meg, even as pain made her grimace. "You *are* a witch."

Then with a scream, Ann's mouth opened wide and fire expelled the soul from within. Meg scrambled back, watching the display with wide eyes. When it finished, she dropped to the ground and tears stung her eyes. She pictured the venom on Azazyel's face and began to tremble anew. She gripped the amulet to her which was now cool to the touch.

"No, I am not a witch. I am a sister."

CHAPTER 25

The burn on Meg's arm began to radiate pain and she grimaced. The amulet had burned through her sleeve and she carefully peeled it back, biting her lip, as part of it had come attached to the burn. There on her arm was a perfect Star of David.

The pain was making her light-headed, and she breathed through her mouth deeply a few times, trying to get the pain under control. Her whole body ached and she could not seem to stop shaking.

Ann lay silently, not moving. Meg crawled over to her. She stared at her chest and was rewarded with its subtle up and down movement. Ann's arm had been branded as well.

Meg knew she needed to leave before Ann awoke. Even without Azazyel present, convincing Ann that she was not a witch would be all but impossible if she woke up to find her here.

Meg grabbed the satchel and looped the strap over her head, wincing as it rubbed against her arm. With one last look at Ann, she hurried back into the woods. Her night was not over yet.

Meg stayed off the roads and cut through the fields. She was careful, keeping her steps quiet in case someone was about. A few times, she heard a branch snap and envisioned Ann flying out at her. Doubts about whether the incantation had been successful plagued her. But she knew it had worked. The power of that moment had been too strong. Azazyel was gone and now only Ann was left, such that she was, which meant there was no impediment to her fulfilling her task.

The book was heavy and her arms ached, but she welcomed the pain. She deserved it and so much more. She pictured the girls, Samuel and the magistrates. *They deserve the most.*

The Followers knew that the life you led here would determine where you went next. The lessons you learned, the kindness you showed; it was all repaid. So she had no doubt that each of those that had willingly taken part in this evil was in for a horrific repayment.

She was human and petty enough to want to see them pay in this lifetime. But that was not going to happen. In this lifetime, the wicked were rewarded and the good were punished. And she knew the stain on the wickeds' souls would take lifetimes to wash away.

She pushed through the trees, seeing her destination ahead. Despite all she had been through, she still believed the plan to bury the book with one of the Followers was the best idea. And she needed to do it now, because tomorrow she had other plans to see through.

She hurried up the hill, knowing the land even in the dark. She had played here. She had laughed here. She had learned here. And now, she would have her final free moments here.

She walked up to the Jacobs family cemetery. Like most in the area, it was rimmed by a wooden fence. She opened the gate, wondering where she would be buried. She walked straight to the newly dug grave.

"Hello, Grandfather."

It had taken Meg hours to dig up the grave. In part because of the work involved but also due to the weeping. When she finally unearthed his coffin, she had been overcome. The shovel had dropped from her hand and she collapsed on the dirt, sobbing.

"I'm sorry. I'm sorry," she cried over and over again.

She lay there, her tears spent as the first rays of sunlight appeared on the horizon. She was exhausted, both physically and spiritually. But her job was not done. Her arms shaking, she pushed herself up as she finished uncovering his grave. Steeling herself, she pulled back the lid.

Her grandfather looked nothing like himself. And the smell. It was unbearable. She held her breath as she climbed out of the grave, her stomach heaving. She knelt on the side of the grave, not wanting to go back in there. Not wanting to look at his face—at what she had put in motion.

You would be responsible for setting me free from my pain. That will be a gift.

She prayed that he was free now. That his sacrifice had wiped whatever stains were on his soul away. Slowly she pulled her satchel over and pulled the book out. The light was so dim it was difficult to make out any of the pages as she flipped through. But as the sun appeared, so too did the images.

The Great Mother, her smile beatific, who was the beacon of light and hope for generations, stared back at her. Each lifetime, she was persecuted. Yet she persisted. She lived. She did what was right, regardless of the consequences. Meg had always been amazed by that strength. But now, now she understood the strength it truly took to sacrifice not just yourself, but those you loved. It was almost unbearable. She ran a finger lightly over an image of the Mother.

"Please give me strength."

Then she slowly covered the book and placed it back in the

box and wrapped it in the leather satchel. She placed it on the edge of the grave before lowering herself back down. Without looking at what had become of her grandfather, she placed the satchel on his chest and then closed the lid.

She placed a hand on the closed coffin. "Thank you, Grandfather." Then she climbed out and began filling his grave. She packed the earth when she was done, but it looked no different than the last time she had seen it in the light. She placed the shovel back against the fence and shed her gloves. Washing up at the well, she took a deep breath, turning her face to the sun.

Then she stepped back and headed into town. The walk went quickly. Everyone gave her a wide berth when they crossed her path. Even though she had not been found guilty, she had been tainted by the accusation. And no one wanted to associate with her lest they too be accused.

The magistrate was arriving at the courthouse when she approached. "Magistrate," she called.

He turned. "Sister Jacobs. What are you doing out so early?"

"I came to speak with you." She took a breath. "I recant my accusations against my grandfather and Reverend Burroughs. They were innocent men."

He reared back, shock splashing across his face. "Are you saying you are guilty of witchcraft?"

"I am saying none of us are or were. You put to death innocent women and men."

His expression hardened. "Recanting will not bring your grandfather or Reverend Burroughs back."

"No. It will not. But at least it will wash some of the stain from my soul."

CHAPTER 26

TWO MONTHS LATER

Once again, Cotton stood outside his father's door. His father had sent him an urgent summons. Cotton was not sure what to make of it. It was not like his father. He smoothed his wig and rapped quickly.

"Enter."

Cotton opened the door and stepped in. "Father. I was—" He paused at the sight of the second man who turned from the window at Cotton's entrance. Cotton bowed. "Governor Phips, it is a pleasure to see you again."

Phips tilted his head, but his anger was etched in every line of his face. "What has happened in Salem?"

"Ah, the trials. They are going well—"

"Well? Nineteen people have been hung! My wife has been questioned. And now I hear you attended and spurred one of the executions."

Cotton faltered mid-step. "Sir, I assure you that—"

"You assure me of nothing!" Phips thundered. "This was supposed to end these ridiculous rumors, but they have just spread further and further. Neighbor is turning on neighbor. You have turned Massachusetts Bay into a battlefield. Bad enough I must fight Indians on the border, I do not need my people fighting amongst themselves."

"But, sir, we are rooting out evil. The Devil—"

Phips strode across the room, glaring down at Cotton. He spoke through clenched teeth. "Are you saying my *wife* should have been questioned?"

Cotton stumbled back. "I—"

"Governor," Increase interceded, "your wife is beyond reproach. A mistake has obviously been made."

Phips glared down at Cotton for another long moment before nodding at Increase. "I am disallowing the spectral evidence. If there are any more witches in Salem, you will have to prove it with tangible evidence. I never should have allowed it to begin with."

"But, sir—"

"Another word, Cotton, and I will have you strung up."

"Me? But I have done nothing wrong."

Phips sneered. "I am sure I could find someone who *dreamed* of you harming them. Get on the right side of this or I will take you down." Phips stormed out of the room, the door swinging wide at his departure.

Cotton stared in shock at the retreating figure of the governor.

"You were looking for the book, weren't you?"

Cotton turned back to his father. "It is a grimoire. It is a beacon of evil. It is—"

"Not what you think. I went looking for information when I heard of your involvement in the trials. I still have some of my father's old books. The book you are looking for is not a grimoire."

"But surely—"

"It is a biography of sorts. It is the story of a woman who has lived throughout several lifetimes."

"Then surely she is a witch and should be—"

Increase shook his head. "You have many degrees, my son, and a lot of knowledge stored in that brain of yours. And yet you remain ignorant of the larger world. That is my fault. But you will hear me now—the tome you are looking for is not about a witch. She is anything but. She is a force of good." He paused. "Have you found any mention of the book?"

"No, Father, but I am sure with time—"

"People are dead. That is on your hands. You will have to answer for that one day. And I suppose I will as well. I have already sent a letter detailing a need for the trials to end. I strongly encourage you to do the same."

Cotton blanched. "But, sir—"

"You are on the wrong side of this, son. Do not compound your crime by continuing down this path. Save the lives you can."

Cotton nodded stiffly. "Yes, sir."

CHAPTER 27

APRIL 1693

Meg had recanted, as she said. And then she'd waited for the day when it was her turn to face Gallows Hill. But the day never came. The governor had finally declared the trials unlawful and brought them to an end. All who had been awaiting trial or execution had been released.

All told, two hundred people had been arrested and accused. Over twenty had died, including those who had passed away in prison. Those deaths were horrible, but it was the betrayals that made neighbor unable to look neighbor in the eye. And Tituba, who had inadvertently started all of this, had been sold again. Meg wasn't sure if that was the worst punishment or the easiest.

The town was shattered. People who'd participated as members of the jury were shunned. Many moved out of town. And Salem's name was now known far and wide. There was even talk about changing the name of the town to signify that it was a different town, that they had divorced themselves from the horror of the last year.

But the horror would not be that easily erased.

She had seen Ann only once since that terrible day. The girl looked haunted, and Meg was sure the memories of what Azazyel had done in her body remained with her. They had messed with powers beyond their comprehension and other people had paid the price for that ignorance. One day, Meg knew she would forgive Ann. But it would not be today.

Meg walked slowly down the lane. It had been almost a year since she had been released. She'd missed spring that year. But now the leaves were changing and there was the scent of new growth in the air. Meg loved the smell of spring—the dirt, the grass, the flowers breaking through. It reminded her she was alive.

Although she had to admit she was having trouble accepting that she deserved to be. She had gone to the court and recanted. And then she had sat in her cell waiting for the executioner to come and take her to Gallows Hill. The truth was, she welcomed it. The ghosts of her sisters, her grandfather, Reverend Burroughs, they haunted her dreams and even her waking hours. She longed for the peace that death would bring.

But it was not to be. Once the governor had disallowed the spectral evidence, the convictions stopped. Without the testimony of the girls there was nothing to convince a jury of a defendant's guilt.

But Meg had a feeling that most of the members of Salem were glad for the change in the rules. The trials had destroyed lives, families, even the sense of safety for the town.

By the end of April, all the charges had been dropped and the court shuttered. The magistrates had left Salem and Reverend Samuel had gone back to being just the town's religious leader. Nineteen people had lost their lives at Gallows Hill. Another four had died in prison, not including Sarah Goode's daughter, Mercy, and poor Giles Corey had been pressed to death.

And then there were the victims that lived but who would never be the same. Salem was perhaps the biggest one. Neighbor could no longer look at neighbor. The town was so splintered, so divided, so cold.

The girls who had been the accusers had gone silent after Ann was restored. At the time, Meg had been unable to feel any sympathy for the haunted look in their eyes. But as a woman with two deaths at her own feet, she felt their pain and hoped they could find a way to smile again, just as she hoped she could find her own way.

But Meg herself was unsure what her next steps were. Her cousin had moved from Boston to stay with her. She was trying to talk Meg into moving to Boston with her. Part of Meg longed to go. To leave all the memories and nightmares behind and start somewhere new.

But she was the last of the Followers, and she had a duty here. As much as she wanted peace, she would not turn her back on what needed to be done. Her sisters had bravely given their lives to protect the legacy of the Great Mother. They had died to protect it. Which left Meg to live to protect it.

She had been making her rounds as she did every weekend, looking in on all the children and grandchildren of the Followers. But she always left this visit for last. It was the most difficult. And yet also the most important. Straightening her shoulders, she made her way up the path and rapped on the door to the small cottage.

Daniel Goode opened the door, relief on his face. "Oh, good. I was worried that perhaps you had changed her mind."

Meg stepped in as he stepped back. "You never have to worry about that. Where is she?"

A flash of melancholy slipped across his face. "Where she always is."

Meg nodded before stepping back outside and making her way

around the cabin. A rocking chair had been set outside underneath the tall maple. A small figure bundled in blankets sat unmoving. A small stool had been set next to the chair.

Meg approached the figure silently, but even if she had shouted a greeting the figure would not have responded. "Hello, Dorcas."

Sarah's daughter did not look up. She continued to stare out over the fields. Meg took a seat next to her and reached for the little girl's hands. Dorcas had been released just after Sarah's death. But she had not spoken a word since. She barely moved. Meg had been worried that Daniel would not be able to take care of her. But he had shown amazing concern that touched everyone in town. Dorcas was a silent, living reminder of the damage done by the trials.

Meg squeezed Dorcas's hand gently and forced a levity into her tone that she did not feel. "It is good to see you. Now, where did we leave off? Ah, yes, I remember. We were speaking about the ring bearer. The one who is called to duty when the Fallen try to beat back the soldiers of light."

Dorcas said nothing as Meg told her tale after tale. But she held her hand tightly. And at the end of the afternoon, Meg began the stories that she knew Dorcas wanted to hear the most.

"And the leader of this incredible group of women was named Sarah Goode. And she stood strong and tall as the world crashed down upon them. Never wavering, never caving in, even as their lives were at risk."

Meg told the tale of Sarah and the Followers' bravery and pretended she did not see the tears that rolled down Dorcas's cheeks throughout the telling. Just as she pretended not to notice the tears that ran down her own. She finished her tale the way she always did.

"And we are the descendants of these amazing women. And we *will* carry on their legacy."

Delaney McPhearson's journey continues in The Belial War. Now available on Amazon

FACT OR FICTION

It goes without saying that *The Belial Witches* is a work of fiction, even though it is based on actual events, so it becomes necessary to determine what is fact and what is fiction. But before we get there, let me say a little bit about why I chose to write *The Belial Witches*. When I was working on *The Belial Plan*, I was searching for a historical incident in America's history that was female-centered. The Salem Witch Trials came to mind pretty quickly.

The more I researched the trials, the more clear the women and the forces arrayed against them became. And as I read about their treatment and the evidence against them, the angrier I got.

And the more I liked the idea of there being a greater purpose behind their deaths... if only that were true. Now on to the heart-breaking fact and fiction:

Numbers. Over two hundred people were arrested and over twenty were killed. The numbers vary slightly depending on the source, but that is the ballpark.

Research. The facts that I have included from the Salem Witch Trials are by no means the extent of the trials. For length, I necessarily had to cut a number of individuals from the story. In some of the research, names and dates varied. This is not a non-fiction

FACT OR FICTION

retelling of the trials, so there will be and are some creative licenses taken.

Names and Susan Osbourne. Sorry about the similarity in names. Apparently, only a handful of names seemed to be used in Salem at the time of the witch trials. There is one name that I switched: Susan Osbourne is actually Sarah Osbourne. But being that Sarah Goode and Sarah Osbourne were incarcerated at the same time, it was frustrating to write and read using both first and last names. As a result, I renamed Sarah Osbourne to Susan Osbourne just to make the reading a little easier. And as explained in *The Belial Witches*, Susan/Sarah Osbourne was sickly and did die in prison.

Cotton Mather. Cotton Mather was a difficult personality to pin down. He was well known for his writings on witchcraft. His role in the Salem Witch Trials is unclear. He wrote about the witch trials in contradictory ways. He argued for the need to root out witches while at the same time arguing against trials. Cotton Mather was one of the leading voices in the fight against the Devil. His father, Increase, was the president of Harvard College. It is unclear if it was his father or Cotton who attended the hanging of Reverend Burroughs and George Jacobs.

Ann Putnam. I liked the idea of one of the girls intentionally manipulating Salem. Ann Putnam seemed to be the ringleader, so she seemed like the most likely choice. Unfortunately for that idea, years after the trials, Ann recanted and apologized. No Fallen would do that. So I needed another way to make her evil yet consistent with history, hence Tituba opening a door.

However, the Putnam family do seem to be identified as a leading cause of the accusations. Those accused all seemed to have crossed the Putnams in some way. The Putnams, by the way, were Rebecca Nurse's neighbors.

Margaret 'Meg' Jacobs. Meg Jacobs was only seventeen years old when she was arrested. She did accuse both her grandfather and Reverend George Burroughs, who had moved out of the area. She later recanted her testimony and sat in jail waiting for her death sentence. But the trials were ended and she was released.

Dorcas Goode. Sarah Goode's daughter was arrested shortly after she was. Sources conflict as to her age, but the oldest age attributed to her was seven. She was reported to have been chained to a wall in a cell for the duration of her incarceration, which lasted months. She never recovered and was unable to take care of herself for the rest of her life. Her father filed a lawsuit on her behalf and won a successful settlement. It was the largest settlement of any of the lawsuits brought on behalf of the victims of the witch trials.

Salem. Salem never truly recovered from the trials. Most of the jurors moved away and the town itself struggled with its reputation. Eventually the town was renamed Danvers, Massachusetts, hoping that the name change signified to the world that they were not the same town that had engaged in the trials.

Main characters. When I was writing *The Bell Plan*, I became fascinated with the witch trials. They were truly a horrible time in American history. In creating *The Belial Witches*, I struggled because everyone I thought would be my main protagonist died early on during this dark period. That is how Meg ended up being our main character.

Sarah Goode. Sarah Goode was disliked in Salem before the trials began. She was opinionated and loud. She did not hold back. She also had a husband who ran through her money and then died, leaving her in debt with mouths to feed. And her second husband was not wealthy. She was known to resort to begging when times got tough.

To be honest, Sarah broke my heart. As mentioned above, her daughter Dorcas was indeed arrested shortly after her and held in chains for months at around the age of five. Sarah herself was pregnant with a little girl, who was born in jail and then died. She was named Mercy.

The quote attributed to Sarah where she prophesized

FACT OR FICTION

Reverend Nicholas Noyes's death is accurate. And the reverend did indeed die fifteen years later, choking on his own blood as a result of a hemorrhage.

The Rights of Women. It was difficult on multiple levels to write *The Belial Witches.* There *were* men accused, but the predominant individuals accused and killed were women. In this time period, they had no rights. They were completely powerless against the forces arrayed against them. They could not even fight back verbally against their accusers because their accusers spoke of their specters attacking them at night. It was only when the governor's wife was charged that he disallowed this spectral evidence and the trials fell apart.

The Accusers. All of the young girl accusers were friends. According to some reports, Tituba did indeed introduce the young girls in her charge to the supernatural. And once the trial began, the number of accusers grew as neighbor turned on neighbor to save themselves.

Publication Schedule. Some people have been kind enough to reach out and ask how many more books will be in the series. There will be three more: *The Belial War, The Belial Fall,* and *The Belial Sacrifice.* I don't have firm publication dates for them but hopefully the first will be out by January 2018.

Before that, however, the second full-length novel in the *A.L.I.V.E. Series, D.E.A.D.,* will be released in June. In addition, *The Unwelcome Trilogy,* will be released this summer. Keep an eye out for them or you can sign up for my mailing list and I'll let you know when they are released.

Thank you again for reading! Until next time,
R.D.

THE BELIAL WAR

BOOK 12

AMAZON BEST-SELLING AUTHOR
R.D. BRADY

Keep reading for a peek at *The Belial War*

THE BELIAL WAR

9,789 BCE

DWARKA, INDIA

The torchlights flickered, throwing moving shadows along the Hall of Knowledge. Tall, thick pillars lined the middle of the room, holding up the forty-foot-tall ceiling. During the day, Yamini loved this room, but in the darkness of night, the shadows seemed to reach for her as she rushed past, her pale student's shift rustling loudly in the quiet of the room.

He comes. Yamini tried not to let the terror overwhelm her. The vision had been the most frightening one she'd ever had. But she needed to keep her wits about her.

"Young Yamini, where are you off to in such a hurry?"

With a cry, Yamini stumbled to a stop, taking a step back as Jagrav stepped from behind a column. The high priest was a member of the Council of the Children, but Yamini did not trust him. She did not like how he looked at the young pages that were being initiated. He said all the right words, but he did not feel them.

She inclined her head. "Learned Jagrav, I did not see you there."

His dark eyes pierced into hers. "Perhaps because you were in such a rush. Is something the matter?"

She forced herself to not look away. "No, Brother. It is just the shadows. I do not like being in here at night."

He paused a beat before responding. "Come now, child, you know there is nothing to hurt you in the Temple of the Children. Unless you have *seen* something that has caused you worry?"

Lying was never Yamini's way. She did not believe when people said that at times there was a reason to lie. That was a reasoning the Sons of Belial used. But right now she could not tell him the truth. "Are you never afraid in the dark?"

He puffed out his chest. "Not since I was a child."

"Perhaps one day I, too, will outgrow these fears." She stepped to the side. "Good evening, Brother."

"Good evening to you as well, Yamini," he said as she passed.

She felt his eyes on her, and she had to restrain herself from sprinting down the hall. She pushed through the tall wrought-iron doors at the end of the room, pausing to glance back. Jagrav stood in the same spot. She gave him a nod before slipping through the doors. Then she sprinted to the stairwell, taking the stone steps two at a time. She flew around the corner. Sister Maya's door was open, a light glowing from inside.

She's still up. Yamini had worried she would have to wake her mentor. This news could not wait. She hurried into the room, and her mentor and friend looked up. In the candlelight, some of the wear and tear of her fifty years was washed away. The wrinkles around her eyes and mouth were less pronounced, and her dark hair streaked with gray looked almost brown.

A smile crossed Maya's face, the lines around her eyes and

chin reappearing as she caught sight of Yamini. "My dear, it is late. Why are you still here?"

"Oh, Sister, I have had a vision."

Maya hurried around the desk, ushering Yamini into a chair. "It will be all right. Whatever you have seen—"

Yamini gripped her hand. "No. They are coming."

∽

The council met as dawn broke. The thirteen elders sat along the long polished stone table at the front of the room. As the group's leader, Maya had the place of honor in the middle.

Yamini had been to meetings before, all of the Children had. But she'd never been to a closed-door meeting. Today it was only the council and their aides, who sat behind the council members, ready for their orders. The only one sitting in front of them was Yamini. Maya stood, addressing the council.

"Yamini has had a vision. Samyaza comes for us." She nodded at Yamini, who stood and recounted the arrival of Samyaza and his followers as well as the destruction that would follow.

"Are you saying Dwarka will not survive?" Ellghad asked.

Images flew through her mind—the bodies of the people she knew and loved floating in water, their faces frozen in horror. Her voice broke. "No, Brother. It will not."

She retook her seat as the council began to debate. Yamini only half listened, her mind replaying what she had seen. Samyaza striding down the Hall of Knowledge, his minions flaring out behind him, cutting down everyone in their path even though they offered no resistance, the giant wall of water washing over Dwarka and pulling it to the bottom of the ocean. Her hands trembled. She clasped them together tightly in her lap.

"But the knowledge must be saved," Jagrav said. "It cannot die with us."

"We should have destroyed the instructions long ago. No one

who wants the power it yields should ever have it," one of the other sisters added.

Yamini started. She knew there was knowledge forbidden from all but the council. She had heard rumors of what it might be, but no one knew for sure. But, of course, that would be why Samyaza was headed their way.

One of the other brothers shook his head. "We don't know that. Perhaps there will be a time when—"

Maya raised an eyebrow but not her voice. "When humans are no longer human? When we do not want more than what fate has provided us? To allow people to awaken the power of a god within others? No good can come of that. The knowledge must be destroyed before Samyaza and his forces arrive."

Jagrav's mouth narrowed to a slit. "And what of Samyaza? How will we protect against him?"

Maya looked at him, shaking her head. "We cannot. If Yamini's vision is correct—and they always are—Samyaza will destroy us all."

"And we will just sit back and allow that?"

"We chose these paths before we ever breathed a single breath. You know that. We are put on this plane of existence to learn, to love, to embrace the beauty of humanity. If this is our destiny, then so be it."

Yamini understood their teachings. She believed them. But when faced with imminent death, it was hard not to wish for some other action.

"We will make sure we evacuate our children and their caretakers. But the rest of us must stay so as to not let Samyaza know they have gone. Not until it is too late."

Maya nodded to her aide, Keshini. Keshini reached down, pulling a box from underneath her stool. Yamini knew the box. It had always been in Maya's room, but she had never seen inside it. Keshini placed the box in front of Maya. With a nod of thanks,

Maya stood and opened it, a faint white glow highlighting her hands.

Maya reached in and pulled out a glowing sphere. At first glance it appeared perfectly round, but then the angles on its face became clear. A murmur rose amongst the table. Yamini couldn't even seem to think for a moment. *It's a belial stone. Maya has had a belial stone all this time.*

The stone was the ancient power source of their brothers and sisters in Atlantis—and also the method of their destruction.

"When Samyaza arrives, we will unleash the power of the stone," said Maya. "We cannot allow him or his followers access to our knowledge. When they are in the center of the city, we will bury them."

"And what of us?" Jagrav demanded.

For the first time that Yamini could remember, Maya sounded tired. "We will be buried with them as well."

No one moved for a moment, but then one by one the priests at the table nodded their agreement. All save Jagrav.

"This is madness," he said. "We should take the knowledge and go before they arrive."

"They will run us down. Now that Samyaza knows where the Omni is, he will stop at nothing. No, this is the only way to protect the world from his power."

"But all our knowledge will be lost."

"Is that truly a bad thing?" Maya asked. "We have the knowledge that would allow someone to gain godlike powers, to become immortal. Tell me, which of the Fallen have demonstrated any kindness or morality with their power? Which of them is a beacon we can point to and tell our children to emulate? This knowledge is not meant for our world. The Belial are not meant for our world. Better we take this knowledge with us than allow it to fall into the wrong hands."

Jagrav's words lashed out. "You condemn all of us to die."

"I condemn all of us to protect this world. That is our mission;

it has been from the start. You do still believe that, do you not, Jagrav?"

Jagrav seemed to finally notice the looks the other members of the council were giving him. The anger slipped from his face, hidden behind a mask of neutrality. But Yamini could still see it lurking behind his eyes. "Yes, of course. I was merely surprised by all this news."

"It is not easy for anyone to face their mortality. Let us all take some time to meditate on what we have discussed here." Maya stood, signaling the end of the meeting. Yamini dropped her quill. Reaching down to pick it up, she saw a pair of sandals stop next to her chair.

She straightened. Jagrav glared down at her. "Afraid of the dark, were you?"

"I . . . I . . ."

"Yamini, I need you," Maya called.

Jagrav whisked past her. Yamini got to her feet, hurrying to Maya's side, a new fear rising in her chest.

⁓

The next evening, Yamini stood on the bridge of the ship along with the other refugees as Dwarka disappeared from view. Four ships had set out, loaded with four hundred people. Four hundred of five thousand. She took a trembling breath, picturing Maya the last time she had seen her. She would never see her again.

No, I will. Just not in this lifetime.

One by one, everyone else drifted away from the railing, but Yamini stayed. She stayed long after the island was out of view. Finally, as darkness fell and a cool wind began to blow, she turned to go inside. Lights shone along the cabins, and hushed voices and the occasional laugh could be heard as she made her way to her room. She would share it with three other initiates. Yamini picked up her pace, suddenly wanting their company. She did not want to be alone.

She climbed down to the second level. Her cabin was halfway down the hall. She pushed the door open, the light spilling out into the hall.

"Did any of you—" A hand slid over her mouth and a strong arm wrapped around her waist, yanking her inside. She struggled for only a minute before she went still. A small cry erupted from her as she took in the sight of her friends, lying on the ground, staring at nothing, long red jagged cuts across their throats. Men she knew stood near them, pulling sheets over them.

"Finish up," Jagrav ordered from behind her. The other men finished rolling her friends up in the sheets, removing them from Yamini's view.

Jagrav leaned down, his lips touching her ear and making her shiver. His voice was a hiss. "If you yell, if you make a sound that draws any attention to this cabin, I will kill you and whoever comes to help you. Nod if you understand."

Yamini nodded.

Slowly, Jagrav released his hand then his arm. Yamini whirled around. "Why?"

"Why? How can you ask that? Your *mentor* dooms us to death while you escape? I don't think so. Besides, we are on a greater mission."

"Wh-what mission?"

"To protect the knowledge of Dwarka."

"But we have brought the books with us already." She paused as the truth hit her. "But that's not the knowledge you want to save. We can't, Jagrav. It's too dangerous."

"What do you know? You are a child."

"But the Great Mother, she chose mortality to save us."

"Perhaps she wasn't as wise as we were taught to believe."

Yamini stared at him in the dim light. His hair was unkempt, sweat dotting his forehead and blood-splashed tunic even though the cabin was cool. His gaze kept darting around the cabin, his lips moving but no words coming out. That's when she noticed the serrated blade in his hand, blood dripping from it in a pool at his side. "What are you planning?"

He smiled, his gaze focusing on her. "To protect that which needs protecting. To bring it back to the beginning."

She frowned. "I don't understand."

"You don't need to."

He sliced the blade across her neck.

Check out The Belial War on Amazon today!

ABOUT THE AUTHOR

Author, Criminologist, Terrorism Expert, Jeet Kune Do Black Sash, Runner, Dog Lover.

Amazon best-selling author R.D. Brady writes supernatural and science fiction thrillers. Her thrillers include ancient mysteries, unusual facts, non-stop action, and fierce women with heart.

Prior to beginning her writing career, RD Brady was a criminologist who specialized in life-course criminology and international terrorism. She's lectured and written numerous academic articles on the genetic influence on criminal behavior, factors that influence terrorist ideology, and delinquent behavior formation.

After visiting counter-terrorism units in Israel, RD returned home with a sabbatical in front of her and decided to write that book she'd been thinking about. Four years later she left academia with the publication of her first book, *The Belial Stone*, and hasn't looked back.

To learn about her upcoming publications, sign up for her newsletter here or on her website (rdbradybooks.com).

BOOKS BY R.D. BRADY

Hominid

The Belial Series (in order)
- The Belial Stone
- The Belial Library
- The Belial Ring
- Recruit: A Belial Series Novella
- The Belial Children
- The Belial Origins
- The Belial Search
- The Belial Guard
- The Belial Warrior
- The Belial Plan
- The Belial Witches
- The Belial War
- The Belial Fall
- The Belial Sacrifice

The Belial Rebirth Series
- The Belial Rebirth

The Belial Spear
The Belial Restored
The Belial Blood
The Belial Angel
The Belial Templar (Coming Soon)

The A.L.I.V.E. Series
B.E.G.I.N.
A.L.I.V.E.
D.E.A.D.
R.I.S.E.
S.A.V.E.

The H.A.L.T. Series
Into the Cage
Into the Dark *(Coming soon)*

The Steve Kane Series
Runs Deep
Runs Deeper

The Unwelcome Series
Protect
Seek
Proxy

The Nola James Series
Surrender the Fear
Escape the Fear
Tackle the Fear
Return the Fear

The Gates of Artemis Series
The Key of Apollo

The Curse of Hecate
The Return of the Gods

R.D. BRADY WRITING AS SADIE HOBBES

The Demon Cursed Series
Demon Cursed
Demon Revealed
Demon Heir

The Four Kingdoms
Order of the Goddess

Be sure to sign up for R.D.'s mailing list to be the first to hear when she has a new release!

Copyright © 2017 by R.D. Brady

The Belial Witches

ASIN (E-Book): B07169X1HH

ISBN (Paperback): 979-8632583008

ISBN (Hardcover): 9798797942955

Published by Scottish Seoul Publishing, LLC, Dewitt, NY

All Rights Reserved. No part of this book may be reproduced or transmitted in any form or by any means, electronic or mechanical, including photocopying, recording, or by any information storage and retrieval system without the written permission of the author, except where permitted by law.

Printed in the United States of America.

Printed in Great Britain
by Amazon